ELEMENTALS 4

THE PORTAL TO KERBEROS

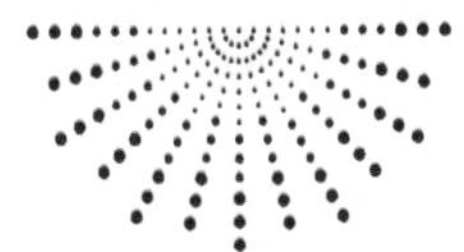

MICHELLE MADOW

ELEMENTALS 4: The Portal to Kerberos

Published by Dreamscape Publishing

Copyright © 2016 Michelle Madow

ISBN: 978-0-578-98859-7

This book is a work of fiction. Though some actual towns, cities, and locations may be mentioned, they are used in a fictitious manner and the events and occurrences were invented in the mind and imagination of the author. Any similarities of characters or names used within to any person past, present, or future is coincidental.

All rights reserved. No part of this book may be used or reproduced in any manner whatsoever without written permission from the author. Brief quotations may be embodied in critical articles or reviews.

CHAPTER ONE

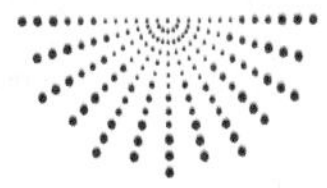

I stared blankly at the spot where Ethan and Blake had been standing a few seconds earlier. I felt empty, as if all the air had been sucked out of my lungs. I couldn't breathe. I couldn't think.

Blake was gone. Ethan had turned on us and taken him into Kerberos—the prison world the Titans had been forced into three thousand years ago after rebelling against the Olympians.

Kerberos was supposedly so terrifying that just being there could drive someone insane in weeks—or days.

The portal to Kerberos had been sealed for thousands of years, until the Olympian comet appeared in the sky a few months ago. Now the portal was weakening, and less powerful monsters were slipping through, including the soul of the most dangerous monster himself—Typhon.

It was supposed to be nearly impossible for Typhon to rise again, because after the Second Rebellion, Zeus split Typhon's soul from his body, locking his soul in Kerberos and trapping his body under Mount Etna in Sicily, Italy. But now that Typhon's soul had escaped from Kerberos, it wouldn't take long for him to reach his body. And on the spring equinox—about six days from now—his mind and body would join and become one. If that happened, he would surely rampage the Earth, destroying all creatures in his path.

Then on the summer solstice, the portal to Kerberos would open and *all* of the monsters locked within—including the Titans—would escape and be free to rule again.

Whether or not we stopped Typhon was a pivotal moment that would determine future events. We'd been *told* this by Nyx, the primordial deity of night itself who could travel between worlds and see all possible futures. If we stopped Typhon, we would have a chance to seal the portal to Kerberos, locking the Titans and all the other monsters inside. If we failed to stop him, we would be unable to close the portal, and war with the Titans would be inevitable.

The world might never recover from the devastation that war would bring.

The only way we could stop Typhon was by bringing the head of Medusa with us to Mount Etna, waiting for the moment he re-joined with his body, and forcing him to look into Medusa's eyes so he would turn to stone. Getting Medusa's head was difficult, and we'd lost one of our own—Kate—in the fight. She'd been turned to stone by Medusa. But we *did* get the head.

Once we used it to destroy Typhon, we would close the portal. Then we would research to discover if there was a way to reverse Medusa's curse.

Kate was one of us, and we wouldn't give up on her until we'd explored every possible way to save her.

But now Ethan had turned on us, taking Medusa's head—and Blake—with him to Kerberos. He'd made some kind of deal with Helios that if he stole the head and brought it to the Titans in Kerberos, Helios would bring Ethan's twin sister Rachael back from the dead and would protect him and his family when the Titans rose again.

Now I stood there, staring at the muddy portal to Kerberos, waiting for Blake to emerge. He would be holding Medusa's head and smiling, he would tell us how he'd burned Ethan to a crisp, and then he would ask when the next flight to Italy was so we could go to Mount Etna and turn Typhon to stone.

I reached for the knife in my boot and waited for

what felt like an eternity, ready to fight in case Ethan came out as well.

But the spot in front of the portal remained empty.

Blake wasn't coming out.

Which gave me only one option—I had to go in there and get him myself.

CHAPTER TWO

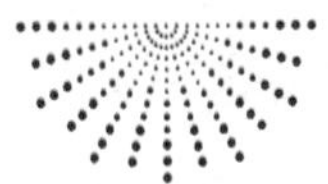

I ran toward the portal, but the air itself pushed against me. I couldn't move. I ran harder, trying to use sheer determination to break through the wall, but it was hopeless.

"Chris!" I dropped my arms to my sides and glared at him. "Stop using your power. Let me go."

"No," he said, and the wind grew stronger, sounding like a storm as it rushed past my ears. "You know what Nyx—and Darius—told us. We can't go in there. It's not safe."

"What if we go in there and can't get out?" Danielle added.

"This is *Blake* we're talking about." I tried pushing against the wall of air again, but I was helpless against Chris's power. I banged my fists against it and screamed. "He's in there, and who knows what he's facing?" I said. "We can't leave him there alone."

"I know," Danielle said. "I agree with you."

"Oh." I looked at her and tilted my head, confused. "Then why aren't you trying to come with me?"

"Because we can't run in there unprepared, with barely any weapons and no idea what we'll be up against," she said. "We need a plan."

"But we can't just leave Blake in there with Ethan," I said, pointing at the portal. "The longer he's in there… who *knows* what's happening to him? If it were me Ethan pulled in there, Blake would have followed in a second."

"I would have held him back, just like I did to you," Chris said.

"What if it were *Kate*?" I shot back, although I looked down and pressed my lips together, regretting my words instantly. "I'm sorry…" I told him, although from the empty look in his eyes, I could tell there was no taking it back. "I didn't mean it."

"No." He sighed and ran his hand through his hair. "You *did* mean it. And I get why you said it. Because if it were Kate, I would try running in there after her, too. But I'm sure that one of you would do everything you could to stop me. Because Danielle's right. We need a plan. So…" He rubbed his hands together, looking back and forth at both of us. "What's the plan?"

I looked to Danielle, since she was the one who had mentioned coming up with a plan in the first place. Chris did the same.

She took a deep breath and stared up at the ceiling, her forehead crinkled as she thought. "Darius, Hypatia, and Jason are all back at Darius's," she finally said, refocusing on us. "We should go back there and tell them what happened. They *have* to know more about Kerberos than we do. They'll help prepare us, and we'll get the weapons we need from the training center so we're ready."

"But how long will that take?" I asked. "We'll have to get there, tell them the whole story… and then who knows what they'll say or do? Every minute we waste here is more time that Blake's in Kerberos, and every minute that he's in there is another minute when he's in danger."

"And it's more time that Ethan has to deliver Medusa's head to the Titans," Chris chimed in. "We *have* to get that head."

"I know." Danielle bit her lip, pacing around the cave. She kept crossing in front of the child Cyclops, now a stone statue in the center. His face was twisted in agony, his eye wide, his mouth open mid-scream.

My stomach twisted from looking at him, so I turned away.

That Cyclops should have been delivered to the

Cyclops's island in the Aegean Sea. Instead, we'd let Ethan use the creature as a test subject for Medusa's head. The head worked. But then, when our eyes were closed, Ethan grabbed Blake and threatened to turn us to stone if we opened our eyes to try to stop him.

I felt like an idiot for trusting Ethan when he came back from Australia and said he wanted to help us fight.

"What if you asked your dad for help?" Danielle stopped pacing, her eyes focused on me.

"Apollo?" I reached for the sun pendant on my necklace, and she nodded, since of course she meant Apollo and not my step-dad, Jerry. "I don't know," I said, twisting the pendant around my fingers. "I've tried to contact him so many times since he sent me the necklace, and it's never worked. I don't think he wants to help us."

It was either that or he just didn't want anything to do with me. Maybe he was so disappointed in me that he'd given up on me. If I felt like an idiot for trusting Ethan, then Apollo probably thought I was an idiot, too.

"Try one more time," Chris said. "It'll only take a few seconds, right? If it doesn't work, we'll figure out something else. But you *have* the necklace, so it's worth a shot."

"Fine," I said. "I'll try. But don't get your hopes up."

I wrapped my fingers around the pendant and

closed my eyes, taking a few deep breaths to get focused.

Apollo, I thought, but then I corrected myself. *Dad.* It felt strange to think of him as that when I'd never met him, but maybe a personal touch would encourage him to listen to me this time. *We—Danielle, Chris, and I—need your help. Ethan just grabbed the head of Medusa and forced Blake to go with him through the portal to Kerberos. He made a deal with Helios where Helios would bring his sister back from Hades and keep him and his family safe in the upcoming war if he delivers Medusa's head to the Titans. He forced Blake with him because he wanted revenge against me for Rachael's death. We want to go into Kerberos to stop him, but we don't have much time, and we don't want to go in unprepared. I know you're busy, but if there's anything you can do to help us, we really need it right now, more than we've ever needed help from you before.*

Unable to think of anything else to add, I let go of the pendant and opened my eyes.

"Well?" Danielle's hands were on her hips, and she watched me expectantly.

Before I could answer, an orb of light as bright as the sun filled the room. It was so intense that I had to shield my eyes and turn away.

After a few seconds, the light faded. Figuring it was safe to look, I lowered my hand, turning back to where the light had been.

Standing in its place was a man as tall as a model, with a lean, sculpted body and hair as blond as mine. In tight jeans, a casual blazer, and a designer scarf, he looked like he'd stepped right off a runway for a hipster fashion show. The only thing that clashed with his outfit was the large sports bag slung over his shoulder. He appeared to be in his mid-twenties, but his skin was so smooth that he could have been ageless. And his resemblance to me was unmistakable.

"Apollo?" I said, my voice cracking when I said his name. "Dad?"

CHAPTER THREE

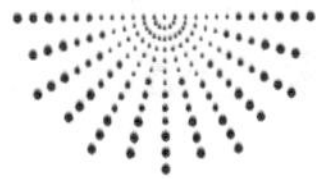

"You called, and I came," he said, as if he hadn't ignored my call every other time I'd tried. "From what I heard, you're in a bit of a bind, aren't you?"

I stared at him, shocked that he was here. I knew he was my father, but it was difficult to actually *believe* it now that he was standing in front of me. Mainly because he appeared to be only a few years older than me. He could have blended in with the college kids who hung out in the city—minus the unearthly radiance that would make him stand out from them all.

Being here with him now, I had no idea what to say. This was the first time I'd ever been face to face with my father. I had so many questions I wanted to ask him. Why did he desert my mom when he learned she was pregnant? Why didn't he tell her the truth about who he was? Why didn't he want to be in our lives? Why didn't he feel the need to let me know that I was a demigod? And why didn't he care about ever getting to know me?

I suspected I already knew the answer—it was because he was a *god*—and family and relationships didn't have the same meanings to gods as they did to mortals. Still, I wanted to hear him say it. No apology could ever take back the years of him being gone, but it would be better than nothing.

But I swallowed down my questions, trying to get ahold of myself. I hadn't called Apollo here so we could have a heart-to-heart. I called him here because we needed his help. And we needed it *now*.

"Thank you for coming." I stood straighter, finally finding my voice again. "We need to go to Kerberos as quickly as possible so we can help Blake fight off Ethan, and bring Medusa's head back to Earth. I tried to run in there the moment they disappeared, but Chris and Danielle stopped me. They said we needed a plan. So… I thought you might be able to help."

"Smart move not running straight into that portal," he said, glancing at it in distaste. "You would have been in for quite the shock when you crossed through."

"We know it's dangerous for mortals to go into Kerberos," Danielle said. "But what about gods? What would happen if *you* went into Kerberos to bring back Medusa's head?"

I twisted around to look at her, shocked. We hadn't discussed asking *Apollo* to go into Kerberos for us. It made sense, of course—he had a better shot at surviving in there than we did—but it seemed presumptuous to ask him for such a huge favor.

Although it wouldn't really be a favor, would it? He needed the Titans to stay in Kerberos just as much as we did. I didn't know what the Titans would do to the Olympians if they escaped and regained power, but I doubted it would be good.

"You're right that if I could enter Kerberos, I would have an easier time retrieving Medusa's head than the three of you would," Apollo said. "But unfortunately—or perhaps fortunately for me—the primordial deities are the only gods who can enter Kerberos. They can cross dimensions without needing to use a portal. No other gods can do that—including the Olympians or the Titans. The portal is weak enough right now that most creatures who reach the entrance can cross through, but their auras aren't anywhere close to as strong as a god's. No gods will be able to pass through until the summer solstice, when the portal is open completely. So my crossing into Kerberos to retrieve Medusa's head for you is not an option."

I almost thanked him for offering if he were able to,

but I stopped myself. Because he hadn't *actually* said he would have done it if he could. He'd just said it would have been easier for him to do than it would be for us. It wasn't the same thing.

"So then we'll go through ourselves," I said instead. "Like I *tried* to do the minute Ethan and Blake disappeared through the portal."

"Your friends were right in stopping you," Apollo said. "And you were right in calling me for help."

"I almost didn't," I muttered, unable to meet his eyes. "You hadn't come any other time I asked for help. I didn't think it would work this time, either."

"I didn't come those other times because while you may have *thought* you needed my help, you didn't truly need it." He held his gaze with mine, watching me closely. "Mortal parents nowadays do everything for their children—but I am not a mortal, and you are not a human child. You're a demigod. And you must know that the relationships that gods have with our children cannot be compared to mortal relationships. We watch out for our children from afar, and it's assumed that our children know that we're keeping an eye on them. But we expect them to fend for themselves. It's the best way that you can grow, so you can become the strongest version of yourself possible. We only interfere if it's absolutely necessary."

I thought it sounded like an archaic and aloof

parenting method, but then again, Apollo *was* thousands of years old. And as he stood there in front of us, his skin so bronze that it appeared to glow with the light of the sun itself, I couldn't forget that while he was my father, he was also a *god*. Our relationship would never be normal.

But I still wished things could have been different between us.

I was afraid to tell him that though, because I had a feeling he would just tell me there was no changing the way things were. And anyway, we had more important issues to discuss, since every moment we spent here was time lost going after Ethan in Kerberos.

"Since you're here now, you must want to help us," I said instead. "Right?"

"Correct." He removed the sports bag from his shoulder and placed it at his feet. "The three of you are right that your best course of action is to enter the portal to Kerberos to take back Medusa's head. You're also right that going in there without the appropriate knowledge and tools would be unwise. So I've come to help you solve both of those problems."

"Great." Chris rubbed his hands together and glanced down at the bag. "If this is anything like the mint Zeus gave me to amp up my power so I could fly the yacht over Charybdis, then I bet it's gonna be good."

"I assure you—what's in that bag is far sleeker than a

mint." Apollo scrunched his nose, as if Zeus's gift appalled him. "But before I present your gifts to you, I need to warn you—Kerberos is a realm accessible from Earth, but it's not actually a *part* of Earth. It's part of a different dimension. Your elemental powers are linked to the Earthly dimension. Therefore, you won't be able to access your abilities while you're in Kerberos."

"What?" Chris's mouth dropped open. "Without our powers, how are we supposed to fight?"

"You're descendants of gods, and Nicole is a demigod," Apollo said. "Fighting is in your blood. Unfortunately, most of your kind has become weak in the past century, growing comfortable in a time of peace and safety. But as you've seen from your training, you pick up on the skills of combat faster than a human ever could. You *can* do this.

"Nevertheless, Kerberos is a deadly place for mortals who have only been training for a few months. Which is why I brought you each a gift that will help you while you're there. But before I present them to you, I must ask you one important question." He paused, taking time to look each of us straight in the eye.

I fidgeted under his gaze, but I didn't break eye contact with him. I was strong. And I wanted him to know that.

He nodded, apparently satisfied, and continued,

"Now that you know your powers won't work in Kerberos, do you still plan on making this journey?"

CHAPTER FOUR

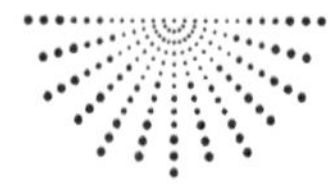

"Yes." I didn't hesitate. "Blake's in there with Ethan—and with who knows *what* other monsters. We can't just do nothing. Plus, we need Medusa's head. We *have* to go in there. We don't have a choice."

"I expected you would say that," Apollo said. "I've observed mortals enough to know that they'll gladly enter hell to save the ones they love, as you're planning on doing now. But your friends don't have the same connection to Blake that you do. Are they willing to risk themselves for him as well?"

"Of course we are." Chris clenched his fists, looking ready to fight. "We're all in this together."

"Plus, if we don't get Medusa's head, the whole

world's going to hell anyway," Danielle added. "So yes. We're all going."

"I'd expected you would say that, but I had to check." Apollo kneeled down to the bag and unzipped it. He reached inside and pulled out something I recognized instantly—the Golden Sword of Athena. "First things first, I thought you would need this," he said, holding the sword out to Danielle. "I dropped by the training center on my way here to pick it up. Why did you leave it there in the first place?"

"We were only coming here to test using Medusa's head on the baby Cyclops," she said. "It was supposed to be easy. We didn't want to risk our weapons scaring the Cyclops before we lured him into the cave."

"Whose idea was that?" Apollo asked.

"Ethan's," Chris said in disgust.

"I'm sure I don't need to remind you to be careful about who you trust." Apollo passed the sword to Danielle, who smiled the moment she wrapped her fingers around the handle. "This sword is yours," he reminded her. "Your ancestor Aphrodite enchanted it into that block of ice for thousands of years, waiting for the day when you would claim it as your own. You should keep it nearby, always."

"Yes," she said, still holding the sword straight in front of her. "I will."

"In addition, I brought a belt and a sheath, since you can't march around Kerberos without a way to carry your sword." He removed that from the bag and handed it to her.

She fastened the belt around her waist and placed the sword inside the sheath, looking every bit a fierce warrior ready to fight.

"Much better." Apollo nodded. "And now, Chris's present." He knelt back down to the bag and pulled out a golden miniature harp. It had a strap around it, presumably so a person could carry it on his or her back. "A golden lyre," he explained, running his fingers over its strings. "I've put an enchantment on it—when it's played, the person playing it will have powers similar to a Siren. When they speak, whoever is listening will believe and do whatever is asked of them."

Chris eyed the instrument skeptically, not reaching out to take it. "And you're giving that to *me*?" he asked. "I mean, it's a great gift, but I don't know how to play any instruments. Especially not a lyre."

"Your inexperience won't be an issue," Apollo said. "As I told you, this lyre is enchanted. You'll be able to play it the moment you lay your hands upon it."

"Cool." Chris's eyes lit up, and he reached for the instrument. "I'll try it now."

Apollo frowned and held it out of Chris's reach. "The enchantment will only last for as long as the lyre remains in tune," he said. "Each time you play it, it will become closer and closer to getting out of tune. So you must be careful to play it only when necessary."

"That makes sense," Chris said. "How many times can I play it before it goes out of tune?"

"I can't say for sure, since it depends on how long you play it each time you use it," Apollo said. "Therefore, I recommend that once your subject has done as you've asked of them, you stop playing as soon as you can. You should also know that it will only work on creatures that can understand English, and that it won't work on gods, as they're too strong to cave into its powers. So if you come across any animals or gods, you'll have to use another means to fight them."

"Got it," Chris said, and this time when he reached for the lyre, Apollo allowed him to take it.

I was slightly jealous when I looked at it. It was beautiful—gleaming as gold as Danielle's sword. Even the strings were made of gold. I itched to play it myself. But Apollo was giving it to Chris, not me, and I had to respect that.

"Thank you." Chris strapped the instrument to his back and stood proudly, looking Apollo straight in the eye. "I'll do everything in my power to protect your daughter when we're in Kerberos. I promise."

"I appreciate it," Apollo said, which was probably the most fatherly thing he'd said since arriving here. "But from what I've seen of Nicole's fighting, she's able to protect herself just fine. And her fighting skills will be even more enhanced with the gift I brought for her today."

Then he reached back into the bag and pulled out the most perfect gift for me.

CHAPTER FIVE

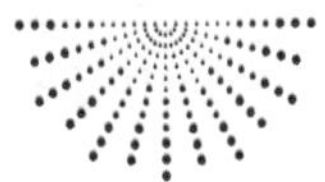

"A golden bow." I gasped upon seeing it, amazed by its beauty. It was so shiny and delicately carved that it made the iron bow I'd been using until now look plain in comparison. "It's beautiful. Thank you."

"This isn't just any bow and arrow set." He pulled out the matching arrows and placed them into the quiver—six of them in all. Like the bow, they were gold, except for the tips, which were a clear, sparkling crystal. "These crystal arrows are exceptionally rare. They will never miss their intended target, as long as that target is in the shooter's range of vision."

"Never?" I asked. "Even if something else gets in the way?"

"If that were to happen, they will divert the obstacle and hit their target," he confirmed. "But you must use them wisely, because the power of the crystal will only work once. Afterward, the crystal will dim, its power gone forever." He handed the bow to me, setting it in my hands. "You must be selective about when you use the arrows, since you will only get six perfect shots."

"I will be," I told him, and with that assurance, he let go of the bow. "But even after the magic of the crystal is gone, I can still use the arrows, right?"

"If you're able to retrieve the arrows, then yes, they're reusable," he said, handing the quiver with the six arrows to me.

I fastened it around my back, tucking the bow in there as well. With the weapon, I felt much more prepared to enter Kerberos. "Thank you for coming when I called today," I told Apollo, not sure what else to say to him. It was strange—despite his being my father, the two of us were still practically strangers. "It means a lot."

"As I said—you needed me, so I came," he said. "But remember that no matter how much you might need assistance in Kerberos, I will not be able to come to your aid while you're there. Not only am I unable to enter the portal—I'll also be unable to hear your call. Once you've crossed through to the other dimension, you'll be on your own."

"Except we'll have our gifts from you, so we won't be *truly* alone," I said, managing a small smile. "Your gifts are extremely generous, and we'll use them wisely. We won't let you down."

"I'll count on it," he said. "As will the rest of the world."

I took a deep breath, hit again with the reality of how the world as I knew it would no longer exist if we failed to succeed in this mission.

We had no other option—we *must* succeed. The world was depending on it. And given the fact that we had less than a week until the spring equinox, we didn't have long to do it.

"One last thing before you leave," Danielle said, and Apollo looked at her to continue. "Darius, Hypatia, and Jason are waiting back at Darius's for us to return from testing Medusa's head on the Cyclops. I don't know how long we'll be in Kerberos, but I suspect it might be long enough that they'll begin to worry—especially if they look for us and find us missing. Is there any way to get word to them about what happened to us and where we went? At least that way they won't waste time searching for us on Earth, and they'll be able to figure out what to tell our families."

"Yes." Apollo nodded. "I can certainly manage that. Now, since my task here is complete and you have your gifts, I must be on my way. Goodbye, and good luck."

He looked at me when he said that last part. Then the glowing orb of light surrounded him again, and when it flashed out, he was gone.

CHAPTER SIX

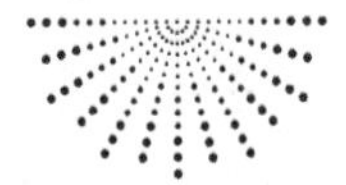

I stared at the place where Apollo—my father—had been standing, thinking about the conversation we'd just had.

"Wow," I finally said, my hand still wrapped around the golden bow. "That really just happened, didn't it? I finally met my father."

"It did," Danielle said. "But you can think more about it later. Because right now, we have to enter Kerberos." She glanced at her watch, concern crossing over her features. "It's been half an hour since Ethan and Blake went through the portal. Hopefully they didn't get too far."

"How far could they get in thirty minutes?" Chris asked. "All we have to do is catch up with them, fight off Ethan, take back Medusa's head, and come back home."

"We can't just *fight* off Ethan," I said, staring straight ahead at the muddy portal. "We now know that he'll do anything to get his sister back—even align himself with the Titans. We can't risk him coming after us again. Remember—he put the gray energy in our drinks before we fought Medusa. If he hadn't done that, Kate would probably still be here today. She's gone because of him, and Blake's in danger now, too. We have no other choice—as soon as we find Ethan, we have to kill him."

"Agreed," Danielle said. "In fact, if you didn't have the heart to do it, I planned on doing it myself."

"And I didn't want to be the first one to say it, but I was thinking it, too," Chris said.

"Good." I gripped the strap of my quiver, glad that they supported me. And while I couldn't speak for Blake, I had a feeling that he would agree with us, too. *If* he hadn't killed Ethan already. In which case, I hoped he'd already grabbed Medusa's head and was on his way back to Earth now.

Unfortunately, Ethan had told us that the Titans were expecting his arrival, so I doubted escape would be that easy. We had no idea what was waiting on the other side. Just looking at the portal—the murky, muddy sludge that swirled on the cave wall in front of us—chilled me to the bone. This portal reeked of evil, and we were about to step right into it.

"So, are we gonna do this or what?" Chris asked, although from the tremble in his voice, I could tell that he was scared, too.

"We need to stop thinking about it and do it," Danielle said. "It's like a Band-Aid—it's better to not think about it too much and rip it off. We have to do the same thing with walking through this portal. Don't think too much about it. Just do it."

"You make it sound like a Nike commercial." Chris laughed. But despite his joke, I couldn't find humor in the situation.

"We'll hold on to each other when we go through, and we won't let go." I held out my hands, and they both took them, their grips tight. "Ready?" I asked, looking first at Chris, and then at Danielle.

"No," she said. "I don't think I could ever feel ready for this."

"Me either," I agreed. "But thank you for stopping me from running in there immediately. You were right—we needed a plan. Now, with Apollo's gifts, we're as ready as we could ever be, considering that not even the gods know what to expect on the other side of that portal."

Then, holding Chris's hand on one side and Danielle's hand on the other, the three of us stepped through the portal to Kerberos.

CHAPTER SEVEN

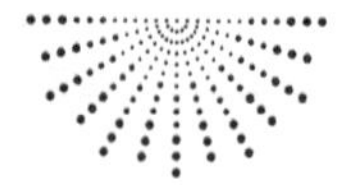

I was prepared for the roller coaster, stomach-flipping sensation I got whenever I walked through a portal, but I should have guessed that this muddy portal to a hell dimension wouldn't be like anything I'd experienced before.

It suffocated me as I fell through, as if I were drowning in quicksand, the sludge covering every inch of my skin. I couldn't breathe. I couldn't move. I was trapped.

We should have arrived on the other side by now.

What if *this* was Kerberos? A constant feeling of drowning in a sludgy nothingness?

If this were all there was, we would never find Blake—we might not even be able to get out of here ourselves.

Just as I started to fear that this was all there would be, my feet hit solid ground again. I sucked in a breath full of air—humid, sticky air, but air nonetheless. I hadn't been able to feel Chris and Danielle's hands while we were in the portal, but now that we were through, they gripped mine tighter than they had before we'd left.

"Well... that was different," Chris said.

"If by 'different' you mean 'terrifying,' then yes." Danielle shuddered and let go of my hand, rubbing her palms over her jeans. "I never want to do that again."

I didn't think she needed reminding that we would *have* to do it again, when we returned home. Instead, I looked around, observing our surroundings.

We stood on a dirt path at the edge of a dark forest. The path split into two—one way led into the dense, tall trees, and the other led to a towering mountain, its peak so high that it rose above the clouds. The sky here was different from our sky—it was a deep, haunted amber. As if the sun were dying.

It was also *hot*. A sticky, wet heat that clung onto every inch of my body, covering my skin like a wet blanket. Sweat already dripped down the sides of my face. Something buzzed by my ear—a fly, I hoped—and I swatted it away. But there was more buzzing, and I looked down at my leg as a giant wasp twice the size of any wasp I'd ever seen on Earth stung me.

"Ow!" I kicked the wasp off of me and pointed at it, flailing around to avoid it landing on me again. "That *thing* just stung me!"

It flew off my leg and landed on Danielle's arm. She took a sharp breath inward and hissed—I guessed it stung her, too.

"Kill it!" she squealed, shaking it off her arm and jumping around to avoid the flying insect. "Now!"

"With what?" Chris asked. "It needs to land on something for us to kill it."

It buzzed around us some more, and then flew away. Once it did, I finally relaxed.

Chris laughed, and I glared at him, clenching my fists to my sides.

"It's not funny," I said, flinching as another fly—or wasp—buzzed past my ear.

"It kind of is," he said, laughing again. "We've fought some of the most terrifying monsters on the planet, and the two of you are screaming like little girls because of a *wasp*."

He waved a hand near his ear—I assumed because of another fly/wasp, and then he flinched, grabbing his hand. "Damn," he cursed, letting go and shaking out his fingers. "That *did* hurt."

"See?" I smiled, glad that he'd experienced getting stung by one of those monstrous insects, too.

"How do you both feel?" Danielle asked. "The bites

feel normal, right? Nothing cold or hot in the place where you got stung?"

"It itches," I said, scratching the sting on my leg. "But no, nothing like that. Why? You don't think those things are poisonous, do you?"

"I have no idea," she said. "They're not from Earth, so I don't know what to expect. But I don't think they're poisonous. My cousin's allergic to bees, and last summer she was stung for the first time while we were hanging out by the pool. She said that it felt like there was cold venom traveling through her body from the place where she got stung. Ten minutes later, her whole body broke out into hives, and we rushed her to the doctor, where they gave her medicine that stopped the reaction. I don't know if it would feel like that for us, since we don't know anything about these wasps, but as long as the bites feel normal then I think we're in the clear."

"Good," I said, fanning my face in a hopeless attempt to cool off. "After everything we've gone through so far, it would be lame to die from an insect bite." Another one flew past my arm, and I skirted away, not wanting to get stung again. Chris jumped as well, which I could only assume was because of another wasp. "If these things don't stay away from us, they're going to drive me *insane*," I said, flinching as it flew past my ear.

"We've only been here for a few minutes, and we're

already being driven insane by insects." Chris shook his head. "No wonder people go mad after a few days of being here."

"We won't *be* here for a few days," I said, swatting another bug off my neck. "Because we're finding Blake, taking back Medusa's head, and then we're getting out of here."

I looked down at the paths, searching for some sort of clue of where Ethan and Blake had gone—footprints, or *something*. Blake should have guessed that we would come after him, and he was smart enough to leave a trail for us. But there was nothing. Both paths looked like they hadn't been used in days.

How were we supposed to know where to go? Splitting up wasn't an option, since one of us couldn't go off on our own. We had to stick together. But if we took the wrong path, we would lose any chance of catching up with them.

"Look!" Danielle said. "Up there!"

I glanced up at where she was pointing, catching sight of two huge orange birds—*pterodactyls*—soaring toward the mountain. Each one held someone in their claws. Even though they were so far away that I couldn't make out details, one had dark hair and the other was blond.

Blake and Ethan.

I reached for my bow, pulling a crystal arrow

through the string. My first instinct was to aim for Blake's pterodactyl to get him away from Ethan, but I couldn't do that—if the pterodactyl dropped him, it would kill him. I had to aim for Ethan. Ethan was likely holding onto Medusa's head, so if I killed him in the air, Blake could grab the head once the pterodactyls dropped them off and come find us. Of course, I had no idea *where* the pterodactyls would drop them off, but we could figure that out later.

I zeroed in on Ethan, steadying my bow and preparing to shoot. I didn't know how the crystal arrows worked—hopefully they would magically *know* where I was aiming to get a perfect shot. But before I let the arrow loose, both pterodactyls rose above the dark storm clouds, disappearing from sight.

Not knowing if they would come back below the clouds again, I shot the arrow anyway, since I'd been looking at Ethan a moment earlier. Apollo said that the arrows only worked when the target was in sight, but Ethan had *been* in sight seconds earlier. If I'd *acted* instead of stopping to think, I would have had him.

I couldn't make the same mistake again. But the arrow was already gone, so I held my breath as it soared up into the air, hoping it would still work.

"Who were you aiming for?" Chris asked, staring at where the arrow had disappeared into the clouds.

"Ethan," I said, wiping beads of sweat off my brow.

"I don't know if it hit him, because he was already in the clouds when I shot. But even if it did and he's dead, the pterodactyls won't let them down until they've reached their destinations."

"Pterodactyls?" Danielle raised an eyebrow. "Those weren't dinosaurs."

"Yeah, they were." I looked at her like she was crazy. "What else could they be?"

"Dragons," she said simply.

I waited for her to laugh, since she *must* be joking, but she didn't. So I laughed instead. "*Dragons?*" I repeated, since that was ridiculous. "No. They were pterodactyls. You know—flying dinosaurs?"

"I know what pterodactyls are." She rolled her eyes as if *I* was the idiot for doubting her knowledge of extinct species. "Dinosaurs were one of my favorite subjects in fifth grade science. That and plate tectonics. But anyway, pterodactyls have pointy heads with beaks, like a pelican without the neck pouch. And their arms are connected to their wings. Dragons have fuller heads with no beaks, and their arms are separate from their wings. Those creatures we saw were certainly the *size* of a pterodactyl, but their features were those of a dragon."

"But dragons don't exist." I lowered my bow, looking up at the sky in wonder. "They're not even part of mythology. They're *fictional*… right?"

"I don't know." Danielle shrugged. "I know a lot about science so I know those weren't pterodactyls, but I don't know every detail about mythology. I mean, I knew everything we needed to know for school, but that was it. I didn't do any further reading."

"If Kate were here, she would know," Chris said.

I looked down at the dirt path, blinking away tears. I was trying not to think about it much, but I couldn't help remembering what Ethan had said to us before disappearing into Kerberos. He'd said that Kate was dead, and that we were pathetic for hoping there might be a way to reverse Medusa's curse.

I was trying not to think about it because I refused to accept it. Kate was part of our team—she was the first friend I'd made when I moved to Kinsley. She'd reached out and gotten me up to speed on everything when I discovered I was a witch. She couldn't be gone. She just *couldn't.*

"She would know," I finally said, pulling myself out of my spiraling, dark thoughts. After all, we couldn't do anything to save Kate right now—but we *could* save Blake. "But it doesn't matter what those creatures are—the important thing is that we saw them flying toward the mountain. So we have a general idea of where they're heading."

"I don't suppose that any pterodactyls, or dragons,

or whatever they were will be stopping by to pick us up, too?" Chris asked.

"Nope." Danielle dug her heel into the dirt path and turned toward the mountain. "Ethan told us that the Titans were expecting his arrival, so I would guess they sent those dragons to him as transportation up the mountain. Which means we only have one option—we have to climb up the mountain ourselves."

CHAPTER EIGHT

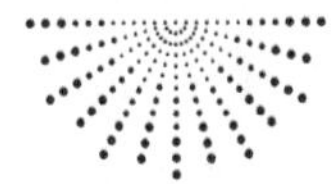

I stared up at the mountain, hopelessness crashing down on me like a ton of bricks. How were we supposed to make it all the way up there? And how would we catch up to Ethan and Blake's head start, since they were flown up there by dragons?

"We'll never make it in time," I said. A wasp buzzed around me, landing on my arm, and I didn't bother brushing it away until after it stung me.

"What do you want to do then?" Chris asked. "Turn around and go back to Earth?"

"No." I sighed and glanced back at the muddy portal. If we'd just been more careful and not trusted Ethan, none of this would have happened, and we wouldn't have to be in Kerberos at all. But we *were* here now, and there was no turning back. So I straightened, waved a wasp away from my ear, and gazed back up at the mountain. "We have to try," I said. "So we need to stop standing around, and start heading up that mountain."

"That's what I like to hear." Chris nodded at me. "And for the record, I wasn't *actually* considering going back. But I knew that if I said it out loud, it would knock you back into your senses."

"It worked." I forced a small smile to show that I appreciated his effort. "I guess we'll just walk toward the mountain. Hopefully we'll find a path up when we get there. How long do you think it'll take?" I looked back and forth between them, hoping that one of them had a general idea.

"Don't look at me." Danielle held her hands out. "I'm not really the mountain climbing type."

"Maybe a day or two?" Chris said. "Or three? I don't know. It depends on a lot of things—if there's a clear trail, how easily we're able to find food and water, etc. We're all in good shape so that won't be an issue, but as for the other things, there's no way for me to know for sure."

"*If* we can find food and water," I said, defeat prickling my skin once more. "On Earth we would probably be able to, but this is a *prison world*. I wouldn't be surprised if there was no food or water on the mountain just to torture us."

Talking about water made me realize that I was getting thirsty. What was the last thing I had to drink? The two glasses of water I'd downed after waking up from my failed attempt to heal Kate. That was hours ago.

Danielle grunted and threw her hands down, and I whipped my head around to look at her, surprised by her sudden outburst.

"What happened?" I asked her. "More wasp bites?"

"No." She huffed again, wiping her forehead with her wrist. "It's so humid here that I thought *maybe* I could pull water from the air so we could have something to drink. But Apollo was right. Our powers don't work here."

"That's too bad," Chris said. "This would be a lot easier if I could fly us up the mountain." He held his hands out and stared forward, his forehead scrunched in concentration. Nothing happened. "Yep," he said, lowering his hands to his sides. "Didn't work."

I didn't doubt them, but I had to try, too. So I placed a hand over one of my itchy wasp bites, closed my eyes, and searched the air for white energy.

There was nothing. I didn't even hit a brick wall—it was just empty. Blank space. A vacuum of nothingness.

My element was gone.

"Nope." I opened my eyes and removed my hand from my arm. "Mine isn't working either."

"Then we only have one option." Danielle stared forward, her eyes glinting with determination. "Let's climb that mountain as fast as possible, find Blake and Medusa's head, and bring them back home."

CHAPTER NINE

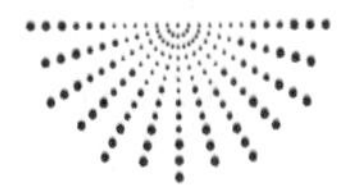

Besides the occasional insect bites and stings, the walk to the base of the mountain was easy, since the path led us straight there. I kept expecting something to jump out at us, but the area around us was barren, and I didn't see any other creatures nearby. But I was still ready to grab my bow at a moment's notice, just in case.

"Do you hear that?" Danielle asked, stopping in her tracks.

"What?" I asked, and she shushed me, which made me instinctively press my lips together.

"Running water," she said. "It's faint, but it's there. Listen."

I stopped to listen, and then I heard it. A light trickling of water from higher up on the mountain. Hearing it made me thirstier than ever.

"If we can hear it, it can't be far," I said, picking up the pace. "Come on."

The path up the mountain was rocky and steep, but since we were all in shape from our intense training, it didn't prove *too* difficult. We wouldn't be able to keep this pace up all the way to the top, but for now, the excitement of knowing there was water ahead kept us going.

We finished stumbling up a particularly steep boulder when something growled up ahead. An oversized, snarling fox. Its tail was down and its lips were pulled back, looking ready to attack.

"Whoa there." Chris held his hands out and stepped back. "Relax, buddy. We're not trying to hurt you. We just want to get up this mountain."

The fox growled again, and then it ran forward, jumping up and launching itself in the air so it appeared to be flying toward us.

Danielle's sword was out in an instant, and she sliced the fox in half. The cut was so clean that there was barely any blood. Just two pieces of the animal, each with a gaping hole on one end, splayed on the ground. It was only after a few seconds that the blood began seeping out and pooling around the corpse.

I glanced around to see if any other animals were around, but we seemed to be in the clear.

"Well, that was different," I said, staring at the remains of the fox. I didn't know much about foxes, but I'd always assumed they were shy. I definitely didn't think they attacked people. So why had it attacked us like that? It was bigger than any fox I'd ever seen on Earth, but it wasn't big enough to feel confident attacking three people.

I had no answer. So we continued on our way, remaining alert in case anything else tried to take us by surprise as well.

We only made it a few steps before another fox wandered out from behind a tree. It spotted us and snarled, its tail grazing the ground, just like the first one. Then another one joined it, and another one behind that one. They all stared at us, blocking our path.

Three of them, and three of us. At least this time it would be a fair fight.

"Come on," Chris goaded them, pulling his knife out of his boot. "You want to fight, even after what just happened to your little friend?"

They all ran forward at the same time, their tails flying behind them as they jumped toward us. I strung a crystal arrow through my bow and shot it straight through one of the fox's hearts. Danielle sliced the fox in front of her clean in half, and I looked over at Chris in time to see him struggling with the last one. It was on him, and his shoulder dripped blood, but I breathed out in relief when he pulled his knife out of the fox's chest. The dead animal dropped to the ground.

"Are you hurt?" I asked, running toward him to check for injuries. He shrugged me off, although I couldn't miss the bloodied holes in his shirt near his shoulder. "You are," I said, pointing to the blood. "How bad is it?"

"It's just a scratch." He rolled his shoulder around, and since he was able to move it, I relaxed. "I'll be fine."

I nodded, since without being able to use my power, I couldn't have even done anything if the injury was life threatening. "First thing to do when we find water is to get it cleaned up," I said. "It might just be a scratch, but you don't want it to get infected."

"Still trying to heal, even when you don't have your powers?" he joked.

"I might as well try to help with what I *can* do," I said.

"First thing I'm going to do when we find water is to take a long drink of it," he said. "*Then* we can clean up this scratch." He dropped his hand from his shoulder and glanced around the clearing. "Hopefully we don't come across any more crazy foxes," he said. "They're really slowing down our progress."

Danielle joined us, handing something to me. "Here's your arrow," she said, and I took it from her, examining it. The previously clear crystal was now murky and gray. "Be careful about how you use the ones that remain," she added. "Use this one if you think you can hit your target without magical help."

"I know," I said, placing the arrow back into my quiver. It felt different from the others—like it was devoid of life. What would happen if I used it? Without access to my powers, would I be able to shoot as accurately as I could on Earth? "I would have gotten it myself, after I checked to make sure Chris was okay."

"I'm sure you would have," Danielle said. "I was just trying to help."

"Oh," I said, still not used to this side of her. "Okay. Thanks."

We walked for a few more minutes in silence, listening to the trickling water get closer and closer. Finally, we pulled ourselves up over another boulder and saw it—a stream up ahead, flowing straight through the path.

"Race you to the water!" Chris said, jumping forward and getting a head start on both of us.

"Hey!" I yelled up at him. "That wasn't—"

I was cut off when a lion jumped onto the path from a ledge above, landing right in front of the water. I skidded to a stop behind Chris, not daring to move. I didn't look behind to check on Danielle, but judging from the fact that I couldn't hear her footsteps, she'd stopped walking, too.

The lion sat down and stared at us, not moving. Its eerie stillness was far scarier than the foxes' snarling. Its eyes were scarily intelligent—as if it had been expecting us.

"Back away slowly," Chris whispered, taking my hand and pulling me back with him. "No sudden movements."

We stopped when we reached Danielle, who was frozen, her eyes wide. I didn't want to use another crystal arrow, but I wasn't sure I had a choice. I didn't want to know *what* would happen if I shot the regular arrow and missed. Surely the lion would attack.

If I used a crystal arrow now, I would only have three left. I was using them quickly—perhaps *too* quickly. I needed to save some for later. But if I didn't use one now, there might not *be* a later for me to save them for.

One perfect shot was all it would take.

I strung the crystal arrow onto my bow and focused on the lion's heart, ready to shoot. But then another lion jumped down to join him, followed by one more. I swallowed, looking around in panic. I didn't have enough arrows for all of these lions. Chris's lyre couldn't do anything since the lions were animals, and it would be too dangerous to fight them with our knives. Danielle had the Golden Sword, but she was only one person. She couldn't take on three lions at once.

How were we supposed to fight these creatures without our powers? They would slaughter us. At the very least, they would injure one of us to the point where we wouldn't be able to make it up the rest of the mountain.

Finally, one more lion jumped down to stand in front of them. He was double the size of the others, and his coat was pure gold. Like the others, he stared at us with intelligent eyes, although he didn't attack. It was more like he and his pack were keeping guard—blocking us from the water and from continuing up the path.

If we kept running into wild animals, we wouldn't make it up the mountain.

"What do we do?" I whispered, making no sudden movements. "Even with our weapons, we can't beat four lions without our powers."

"That's not just any lion," Danielle said, her sword up and ready. "It's the *Nemean* lion. We had a test last semester about Hercules's twelve labors, and the lion was one of them. His golden fur makes him immune to weapons. The only way Hercules was able to kill him was by strangling the lion to death with his own hands."

"Is it immune to the Golden Sword and the crystal arrows?" Chris asked.

"I don't know," Danielle said, taking a step backward. "But for now, he and the others don't seem to want to attack us—just to stop us from going any further. If we try to use our weapons against him and they don't work..."

"Then we'll provoke him into attacking," I finished her thought. "And the other lions as well."

"Exactly," she said. "And even with the Golden Sword and crystals arrows, I doubt that a fight between the three of us, three lions, and the Nemean lion would end well."

I nodded, since I'd already come to that same conclusion.

"So what *do* we do?" Chris asked. "Turn around and lose even *more* time?"

I stared back at the lions. They watched us closely, as if waiting to see our next move. So I stepped forward. The Nemean lion took a step forward as well, his eyes level with mine. He looked ready to pounce. I took a step back, and while it was hard to say for sure, it seemed like the lion nodded. As if he was telling us that if we retreated, he and the others wouldn't hurt us.

"I don't like this any more than you do," I told Chris. "But we're not going to be any use to anyone if we're dead. And this mountain's huge—this can't be the only path up. There has to be a safer way."

"For once, you're thinking sensibly," Danielle agreed.

I rolled my eyes, figuring her comment needed no response, and the three of us took a few more cautious steps backward. The further away from the lions we got, the more they relaxed. They sat down, watching us, and the Nemean lion licked his paw. It was hard to say for sure, but I was pretty sure that he smiled.

They were letting us go. Relief flooded my veins at the realization that we wouldn't have to fight them, and I breathed easily for the first time since the lion had jumped into our path. We moved farther and farther away, and as much as I hated running away from a fight, I knew we'd made the right decision. After all, we were no use to anyone if we were dead.

Not wanting to test our luck any further, we finally turned around, not looking back as we hurried down the mountain.

CHAPTER TEN

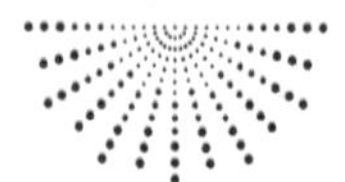

The lions didn't follow us—no more foxes jumped out at us, either—and once we reached the bottom of the mountain, we sat down on a stone to take a breather and decide what to do next.

I looked around the dismal brown landscape, trying to get a better idea of our surroundings. The dirt path we'd taken from the portal was the only obvious way up the mountain. All around the path was a barren wasteland full of sharp, jagged boulders. We *might* be able to trek through them, but it wouldn't be easy, and it would be near impossible at night. But what choice did we have? The path was too dangerous. We *had* to break from it to find an alternate way up the mountain.

"We might as well get going." I jumped off the rock

and brushed off my palms. "We're not getting anywhere by sitting here doing nothing."

"We should have taken the bodies of those foxes that we killed on the mountain," Chris said, not moving from his seat on the rock. A fly buzzed around his ear, and he didn't bother waving it away. "At least then we would have something to eat."

My stomach growled, and I wrapped my arms around it to silence it. Why hadn't Apollo thought to give us some food along with our weapons? We had a while before keeling over from starvation, but our strength wouldn't last forever if we didn't find something to eat.

"Do you know how to cook a fox?" Danielle shot back at Chris. "How to skin it, and how to know which parts of it to eat? And what about starting a fire? Do you know how to do that without a lighter?"

"I have my knife." He held it up, the blade glinting in the rays of the dying sun. "We could have figured the rest of that stuff out. It's better than starving to death."

"We're not going to starve to death," I said, although I had a feeling that I was trying to convince myself of that as much as I was trying to convince him. "And we're not going back up that path. The lions might not let us go twice, and who knows what other animals will try to attack? We have to find another way. Come on."

I stepped off the path, maneuvering myself along the

cragged rocks. Chris and Danielle followed in my footsteps, saying nothing.

We stumbled along for ten minutes—our progress was slower than it had been on the path, but at least it was progress. Danielle used the Golden Sword as a walking stick. Chris and I didn't have that luxury, and there were no sticks anywhere near us, so we had to make our way on our own. So far, I'd only lost my footing once.

I panted as I continued on, cursing the lions for stopping us right before we'd reached water. Couldn't they have waited until *after* we had something to drink?

I suppose that would be too much to expect from a hellish prison world.

To distract myself from my thirst, I kept glancing at the mountain, hoping to spot another path. Everything I'd seen so far was too steep to reasonably climb. But we still had a while to go, so I tried not to lose hope.

I turned my gaze ahead and saw something strange in the distance—a fuzzy, gray blob about the size of a human. "Do you all see that?" I asked, stopping to point at the shadowy blob. "I'm not hallucinating, am I?"

Danielle looked at where I was pointing and raised her sword. "If you're seeing a shadowy blur that's coming closer to us at a speed we could never outrun, then no, you're not hallucinating," she said. "What *is* that thing?"

"I don't know." I pulled out a crystal arrow and strung it onto my bow, even though I had no idea where to aim to injure the thing up ahead. So I removed the crystal arrow and took out the used arrow instead, shooting it at the blob. The arrow disappeared into it. I stood there, transfixed, trying to see where my arrow could have landed, but it was as if it had become part of the shadow itself.

The shadow stopped about twenty feet ahead of us, and in less time than it took to blink, a person stood in its place. A guy a few years older than us, to be exact—dressed in black jeans, a leather jacket, and combat boots. He had dark hair, and a face so perfectly sculpted that he would make even Jason Flynn—one of the most famous movie stars in the world—pale in comparison. He carried a small black pack on his back and my arrow in his hand, but that was all he seemed to have on him.

I strung a crystal arrow through my bow and pointed it at his heart. Danielle held out her sword, and Chris had his lyre ready.

I *should* have shot the guy—or thing, or whatever he was—with the crystal arrow immediately after he shifted to human form, but he didn't make a move toward us, so I held back. I didn't think that any creatures in Kerberos could be trusted, but if this guy wanted to kill us, wouldn't he have done it by now? *Especially* since I'd already tried shooting him once?

"You can lower your weapons." He tossed my used arrow to the ground in front of my feet and held his hands out. "I'm here to help you."

"Why should we trust you?" I remained focused on him and didn't make a move for the discarded arrow, ready to shoot the crystal arrow through his heart at a moment's notice.

"Do you have much of a choice?" He smirked, as if he already knew the answer to the question. "You're wandering around Kerberos with no idea where you're going. Since you're traversing the Badlands—and judging by the bite on Chris's shoulder—you've already discovered that wild animals block the fastest route up the mountain. I'm going to guess that you're searching for another way up, but you're looking in the wrong place. And even if you *do* discover the correct path—which I doubt you will on your own—the chances of you making it to the top of the mountain alive are slim at best. Which brings me to the reason why I'm here—to be your guide."

I stood there for a few seconds, processing everything he'd said. He couldn't be telling the truth. Because no creature from Kerberos was on our side… or at least I didn't *think* they were. After all, they had every reason to want the portal to open, and we had every reason to want it closed. Which made us enemies with everyone here.

Whoever this guy was, there was no way he was here to help us. And if he thought he could trick us that easily, he was wrong.

"How do you know my name?" Chris finally asked.

"If you lower your weapons, I'll tell you," he said.

I glanced at Danielle, who like me, made no move to lower her weapon.

"No." Danielle leveled her gaze with his, holding her ground. "How about this—as long as you stay where you are, we'll promise not to shoot you while you answer our questions."

"Feisty." The man smiled. "I like it."

She raised her sword, which only made his smile grow.

"We know better than to trust anyone from Kerberos," she said. "So go on. Tell us who you are, and how you know Chris's name."

"It's not just Chris's name I know," he said. "I know yours, too, Danielle. And yours, Nicole." He looked at me when he said my name, his dark eyes sending chills down my spine. "And you're right to not trust anyone from Kerberos. Trusting anyone from here would be pretty stupid."

"So then why do you expect us to trust you?" I asked.

"Because I'm not from Kerberos."

I waited for him to continue. When he didn't, I took

the bait. "Where are you from, then?" I asked, not having the patience for whatever game he was trying to play.

"I am from Chaos itself," he said, as if we should understand what that meant. "More specifically, I am Erebus—the primordial deity of darkness, sent here by Nyx to guide you through this prison world."

CHAPTER ELEVEN

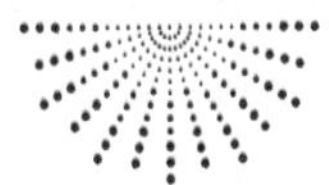

"Why did Nyx send you?" Danielle narrowed her eyes, not looking like she believed a word he said. "Why wouldn't she just come here herself?"

"Excellent questions," Erebus said. "And there are two reasons. First of all, there's an issue on another planet right now that needs Nyx's undivided attention. Don't bother asking for more information on that situation, because that's all I'm allowed to tell you. And secondly, I'm much more familiar with Kerberos than Nyx is. She doesn't spend much time here—she doesn't like it here very much. I, on the other hand, have no issue watching creatures suffer in the most gruesome ways imaginable, so I come here quite often. Which makes me more suitable to be your guide."

"If you like suffering so much, then why help us at all?" I asked. "Why not let the Titans escape, and watch them destroy the Earth?"

"Would you believe me if I told you it was to make Nyx happy?" he asked.

"No," Danielle said, tightening her grip on her sword. "Why do you *personally* want to help us?"

"Fine." He chuckled and held his hands up. "You're right. Making Nyx happy is a plus I get from helping you, but it isn't the reason *why* I'm helping you. The reason why is this—you mortals are so entertaining, it would be a shame to have you wiped out by the Titans. The technological advances that the mortals on Earth have created in such a short amount of time are incredible—you're close to making some remarkable discoveries about what exists beyond your planet. To have your race obliterated now would be hugely disappointing. Sure, it would be entertaining while it was happening, but the Titans would crush you so quickly that it would be over before I could get any enjoyment from it even starting. Therefore, I'm taking Nyx's request to heart. I can't technically *interfere* in your mission, but I'll do what I can to guide you through Kerberos alive. Because while I know you don't want to admit it, without me, the three of you have no chance in hell. And I mean that quite literally, since Kerberos is worse than Hades itself."

"Great," I said, still not lowering my bow. "If you want to help us, create a portal to the top of that mountain, so we can save Blake, grab Medusa's head, and get out of here."

"I'm afraid I can't do that," he said. "It would be too much of an interference. Like I said—I'm here to *guide* you, not to interfere and make this easy for you. Mortals must *earn* success, not have it handed to them by the gods. But I will remain by your side for as long as you need me with you on your journey."

"But how can we trust you?" Danielle asked, her sword still raised. "How can we know that you're not pretending to be who you say you are, and that you're not actually some creature in Kerberos who's lying to us to gain our trust?"

"Because no creature from Kerberos has had any contact with Earth in three millennia," he said. "And of the ones who escaped, only three returned—the harpy, Orthrus, and the siren. But I know that Nyx came to you recently to warn you about Typhon's soul escaping Kerberos. She visited you on Earth, *after* those three creatures I mentioned had returned, so I would have no way of knowing that unless I am who I say I am—a primordial deity, sent here by Nyx to guide you through this dimension."

"Or you could have read our minds," I said. "Or you

could have already found Ethan and Blake, and coaxed that information out of them."

"I could have." He spoke so calmly, as if the three of us weren't aiming weapons at him, ready to kill. "But I didn't. I am Erebus, and I'm here to guide you through Kerberos. You can accept my help or not, but I would advise that you accept it, because without it, you will surely die. And I don't think you need reminding that each second we spend here discussing this is one second closer to the spring equinox." He paused, allowing that to sink in. "But in the end, this is your decision, and I will not force my help upon you. So I will ask this of you once, and I advise that you choose wisely. Do you accept my help, or do you not?"

I didn't lower my weapon, but I didn't shoot the arrow, either. If this actually *was* Erebus, and if he was being truthful, we would be stupid to turn him down. After all, it was already apparent after our failed trek up the mountain that we wouldn't get far in Kerberos without being killed.

But what if this *wasn't* Erebus? What if this was a monster that was *pretending* to be Erebus so he could gain our trust, bring us to who knows where, and trap us and torture us there?

I was about to request to talk with the others alone when Chris started to play the Golden Lyre. Like

Apollo had promised, Chris played like a pro, even though he didn't have experience on any instruments at all. His fingers clearly plucked each note, dancing across the strings to create music so perfect and beautiful that it brought tears to my eyes. If I didn't know any better, I would think that Apollo was playing the song himself.

"If you want us to accept your help, then run as far away from us as you can manage and never speak of us or come near us again," Chris said, the music accompanying his every word.

I glanced at him—making sure to keep my arrow aimed at Erebus—shocked at what he was saying. "What are you *doing*?" I hissed, wanting to smack him for being such an idiot. I would have, if I wasn't holding onto my weapon.

"Stop talking," Danielle snapped at me. "Let Chris do what he needs to do."

I clamped my lips shut, surprised at her outburst. Apparently both she and Chris had gone mad.

Finally, Chris stopped playing the lyre. He lowered it and raised an eyebrow at Erebus, as if challenging the god to see his next move.

I expected Erebus to turn around and run to the end of Kerberos, never seeing him or hearing from him again. Instead, he cocked his head at Chris and laughed.

"Have you lost your mind?" he asked Chris. "Why would I do as you said if I'm here to help you? Which, for the record, I am."

"Good job." Chris nodded. "You passed the test."

"I know." Erebus smirked, as if he knew everything. Which, if he was a primordial deity as he claimed, he likely did. "Apollo's Golden Lyre will convince anyone to do as they're told, unless they're an animal or a god. Since I'm a god, I'm immune to its effects. But if I were a monster here to trick you, I would be running for the hills, and the three of you would never see or hear from me again. Smart thinking," he said, nodding at Chris. "I'm impressed."

"Thanks," Chris said sheepishly, slinging the lyre around his back. "I try."

"It *was* a good idea," I said, feeling stupid for not figuring out what he was doing earlier. "But the Titans are here in Kerberos, and they're all gods. So they would be immune to the lyre's effects, too. How do we know that Erebus—or this god who *claims* to be Erebus—isn't actually a Titan?"

"The Titans are all trapped on the top of that mountain." Erebus pointed to the mountain that we'd seen Blake and Ethan flying toward, the top of it hidden by a mass of dark storm clouds. "But more importantly, if I were a Titan, the three of you would be dead by now."

"He has a good point." Danielle lowered her sword, holding it to her side. "I think we should trust him."

"He passed my test, so I trust him, too," Chris said.

"Which leaves Nicole," Erebus said, his dark eyes so intense that it felt like he could see straight into my soul. "So, child of Apollo," he continued. "What will it be?"

CHAPTER TWELVE

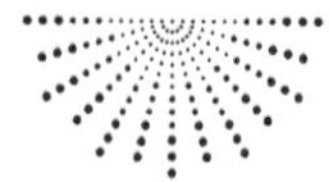

I didn't move from my stance, holding my arrow steady and my gaze with Erebus's. Did I trust him enough to follow him through Kerberos? He was clearly a god—if he wasn't, he wouldn't have been immune to the effects of the Golden Lyre. And I had a gut feeling that he was right—if he were a Titan, he *would* have killed us by now. So, no matter who he was, he didn't want us dead. At least not immediately. And since it seemed like most creatures and monsters who resided on Kerberos *did* want us dead, it would be stupid to deny the help of a god who claimed that he wanted to help keep us alive. Plus, without our powers, we were weaker than ever. We *needed* his help.

"Fine." I lowered my bow, removing the crystal arrow and placing it back in my quiver. I grabbed the used arrow at my feet and put it away as well. "I accept your help, too."

"Wonderful," he said, rubbing his hands together. "Now, as you already know, Ethan has taken Medusa's head to the top of the mountain. Your friend Blake is with him as well."

"I tried to shoot Ethan while he was in the air," I interrupted. "Do you know if the arrow hit him?"

"I'm not supposed to supply you with information you should discover for yourself, but I suppose it won't hurt this one time," he said. "No, your arrow did not reach Ethan, as he was already hidden by the clouds when you released the shot."

"So he's still alive." I frowned, letting go of the hope I'd been holding onto that perhaps my arrow had hit its target.

"That's for you to discover once you reach the top of the mountain," Erebus said. "As you already found out, the quickest, most obvious path up the mountain is also the most deadly. If you had been stubborn and tried to continue, death would have been imminent—even *with* the enchanted objects gifted to you by Apollo. But, as you suspected, that path is not the only way up the mountain. There's another way—although given the direction you're currently heading, you're nowhere close to finding it. It's a safer, more meandering path that will take us through multiple realms of Kerberos.

However, even though it's safer than the direct route, it's still far from *safe*. You will come across monsters and horrors that no longer exist on Earth. You will be exposed to some of the same terrors that monsters have experienced in Kerberos for thousands of years. You would not survive without me, but with me as your guide, you at least stand a chance. It will not be easy, but it's your only option if you wish to succeed on your quest. Are you ready to face the challenges ahead?"

"Yes." I nodded, since at this point, what choice did we have? I would face anything to save Blake. "I'm ready."

"I am, too," Chris said.

"As am I," Danielle said. "But I do have one question."

"Ask away." Erebus motioned for her to continue.

"Ethan and Blake were taken up the mountain by dragons," she said. "Wouldn't it be a lot faster if we could find dragons to fly us up to the top of the mountain as well?"

"Yes." Erebus nodded. "It would. And that's precisely part of my plan, although I didn't think it necessary for you to know until it happened. But since you asked so nicely, I suppose I can tell you now. Dragons reside midway up the mountain, and they're rather fickle creatures. The ones who retrieved Ethan and Blake were sent to this spot by Helios. You see, the dragons in question are Helios's Solar Dragons, who pulled Helios's chariot across the sky. They follow Helios's orders—or the orders of anyone working for Helios—because he is their master. With the portal weakened, Helios must have been able to get a message to the dragons to find Ethan and Blake and fly them up the mountain. The path we're taking up the mountain will lead us to the Lair of the Dragons. A ride from the dragons is the only way to the peak, and while dragons are inherently selfish creatures, they'll do anything for a price. Agreeing on that price will be for you and the dragons to negotiate."

"We'll figure out something," Danielle said, her eyes blazing with determination. "If a ride from the dragons is the only way to the peak, then we *have* to get them to cooperate."

"I respect your willpower," Erebus said. "But be warned that a deal with the dragons will require a sacrifice. However, we have quite a while until we reach them, and I'm sure you don't need reminding that time is of the essence. Shall we be on our way?"

"Of course," I said, and while I still wasn't positive that Erebus could be trusted, the three of us followed him back to the path through Kerberos.

CHAPTER THIRTEEN

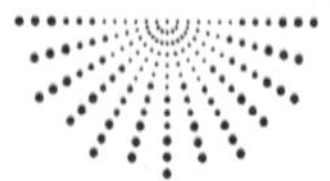

Erebus led us across the cragged rocks and back onto the dirt path—I'd apparently been leading the group in the completely wrong direction. Since the path only led two ways—toward the mountain and back to the forest—I assumed Erebus would walk us along the rocks on the other side of the path. Instead, he turned around and followed the path back to the forest.

"In case you didn't notice, the mountain is that way." I pointed over my shoulder. "Why are we walking *away* from it?"

"I know where the mountain is." Erebus let out an agitated breath and rolled his eyes. "It's a *mountain* for crying out loud. It's kind of hard to miss. But as I already told you, the route we'll be taking is a meandering one that will lead us through the realms of Kerberos. In case you don't understand what that means, the definition of meandering is—"

"Winding," Danielle interrupted, stopping to wipe some sweat off her forehead. "Twisty. Bendy. Curvy. An indirect course."

"Precisely." Erebus nodded at Danielle, his eyes gleaming with what seemed to be *respect*. Danielle just tossed her hair over her shoulder, her lips curved up into a small smile.

"I know what meandering means," I said, annoyed that both of them apparently thought I was missing a few brain cells. "I just thought we would be meandering *toward* the mountain and not *away* from it."

"We must first go away from the mountain in order to eventually head toward it," Erebus said. "When you accepted my help, I thought that meant you trusted me not to lead you astray. Do you doubt me now?"

There *was* a part of me that still questioned him, but since he was the one person in this hell dimension who seemed to want to help us, it would do me no good to tell him that now. "No," I said. "Of course not. Sorry."

Chris slapped away another wasp, but from the pained look on his face, it hadn't been enough to stop him from getting stung. "Is there any way to stop these wasps from biting us?" he asked. "That was probably the tenth time I've been stung, and it itches so bad that it's driving me crazy."

I felt his pain. I also had multiple stings all over my body, and the more I scratched, the itchier they became. Still, while scratching made the bites worse, they burned so bad when I didn't scratch them that I couldn't resist giving in, even if the relief was only temporary.

If Erebus had a way to make it stop, then I was all ears.

"The flies and wasps are part of the torture inflicted by the Badlands—the realm in Kerberos between the mountain and the forest," Erebus told us. "They will sting and bite you no matter what. You can lessen it by not irritating them by swatting at them, but it will not stop them completely. But as I'm sure you noticed, the flies and wasps disappeared once you started up the mountain. They will do the same once we enter the forest."

"You mean that dark, creepy jungle of a forest that we saw when we stepped through the portal?" I asked. "We're going in *there*?"

"Yes." Erebus nodded. "That's precisely where we're heading."

"How's that supposed to be any better than the mountain?"

"The forest will not be an agreeable journey by any means," he said. "But trust me—it's not deadly like the mountain. It won't cause you any physical harm. It's *unpleasant*, but not deadly."

"How so?" Danielle asked.

"You'll see when we get there," he said. "There won't be any creatures to fight, so you needn't worry about that. I'll tell you more once we're closer, but you'll be fine as long as you remember this one important fact—whatever you hear in the forest isn't real."

With that, he turned around and continued down the path. He tugged at the straps of the pack on his back, and I contemplated asking him what was inside, but I stopped myself. After all, Erebus was a *god*. If he wanted us to know what was in the pack, he would tell us. I also had a feeling that we'd annoyed him enough since first meeting him, and I didn't want to push his patience further.

He continued to lead us down the path, and we followed, not saying a word. The only sounds were our footsteps and the buzzing of the flies and wasps that bit and stung us no matter how little we swatted at them. The hot, muggy air created a layer of sweat over every inch of my skin. My hair was wet with sweat even after putting it up. I was getting thirstier and thirstier, but I held onto hope that we would find water soon. Until we did, there was no point in complaining. All we could do was continue on.

The path crested over a hill, and as we ascended I saw the trees in the forest waiting ahead. A dark haze surrounded the forest, and I couldn't imagine the horrors that waited for us within. But I pushed away my fear and focused on putting one foot in front of the other, reminding myself that each step forward was one step closer to Blake.

We reached the top of the hill, and Erebus held his arms out, stopping us from proceeding.

"What?" I asked. "Why are we stopping?"

"Shhhh," he said, facing forward and not looking at me. "Listen."

I doubted that my sense of hearing was any match for his godly one, but I did as he said anyway, closing my eyes so I could focus on the sounds around me. It didn't take long to hear the thunderous footsteps, getting louder and louder by the second. They were quick—whoever was making them was running. And they were so heavy that the ground vibrated under my feet.

I opened my eyes as a big-boned, troll-like creature at least three times the size of a human ran out of the forest. He was followed by another, and then another—there must have been five of them in all. They each carried a wooden bat large enough to squash us like flies.

And since they were following the path, they were heading straight toward us.

CHAPTER FOURTEEN

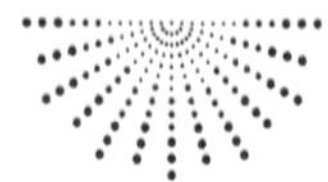

My heart jumped into my throat as the giants ran out of the forest, and I glanced around, looking for somewhere to hide. But since we were in a rocky, desert wasteland, there was nothing nearby that would give us cover. And since there were more of the giants than there were of us, we wouldn't be able to fight them off without our powers.

"Chris." I spoke louder, so he could hear me over the rumbling footsteps of the giants. "Get your lyre ready."

"Already on it," he said, and sure enough, when I turned to look at him, I saw his lyre out and ready to play.

"You won't need to worry about that," Erebus said, his voice annoyingly calm. "Just watch."

Was he going to fight the giants for us? I thought he

wasn't "allowed" to interfere like that, but hey—if he chose to do it, I wouldn't complain. We needed all the help we could get. So, since he was a god, and I trusted him not to tell us to watch the giants if we actually needed to be running for our lives, I did as he said. After all, if he changed his mind and decided *not* to help us, Chris still had his lyre. He could use it to convince the giants to run in another direction and forget they ever saw us.

But none of that was necessary. Because instead of continuing toward us, the first giant hunched over and ran straight through the portal. One second he was there, and the next second he was gone. The rest of them followed his lead until none of them were left. Their pounding footsteps were gone, leaving an eerie silence in their wake.

"They all ran to Earth." I stared numbly at the empty path ahead of me. "Straight to Kinsley. And none of us are there to stop them. Our *families* are there, and now they're at the mercy of those… things." I whipped my head around to look at the others, and pointed at the portal. "We have to go back," I said. "When we're back, we'll have our powers. And then we'll be able to kill those monsters."

"No," Chris said, holding his arm out to stop me. "We can't go back."

"Yes, we can," I argued. "It won't take long. We'll go

through the portal, kill the giants, and then come back here to continue on. Those giants might be big, but they didn't look very smart. With our powers, we shouldn't have much trouble fighting them." I looked at Danielle, hoping she would agree with me. "You're the final vote," I told her. "Should we go fight the giants, or let them run free through our home?"

She looked back and forth between me and Chris, her expression guarded. "I don't know," she finally said. "Our families are in danger, and I hate that. But there are protection spells around their houses, and they know to stay inside. If we lose time while fighting the giants, or worse—if anything happens to us while fighting them—we risk failing our entire mission." She took a deep breath, sheathed her sword, and turned to Erebus. "You're the god, and our guide," she said to him. "What do *you* think we should do?"

"At least one of you has the common sense to ask for my opinion." He spun his knife around—he must have gotten it from his bag—and balanced it on the tip of his index finger. Somehow it didn't draw blood. Once it finished spinning, he caught it with his other hand and continued, "I can't make your decisions for you. But I *can* let you know that the giants are not the only ones to escape. Word of the portal is spreading, and as it weakens, more creatures are able to pass through. The giants are not the first to pass through since you've arrived here, and they won't be the last."

He didn't need to say more for me to know that we couldn't go back through that portal. I think I'd known that from the moment the giants escaped. I liked the *idea* of being able to go back and fight them, but if we went back to fight every monster that escaped through the portal while we were in Kerberos, we would likely never succeed in our mission.

Plus, what if the lost time resulted in something terrible happening to Blake? We *had* to get to him as quickly as possible. Every second lost was another second he was at risk.

I wouldn't be able to live with myself if he didn't make it out of this okay.

"Even if we go back for the giants, we can't go back for every group that escapes while we're here," I resolved, my heart dropping as I looked at the portal. "If we go back for the giants, we'll be losing time here. It makes the most sense for us to continue on and get Medusa's head as quickly as possible. In the meantime… let's hope that Darius is making sure that our families stay safe."

"I'm glad you're seeing this sensibly now," Danielle said. "Remember—Apollo promised he would go to Darius's to warn him. Darius is smart, and he has

Hypatia and Jason with him, too. They'll do everything they can to keep the town safe."

"I know," I said, although it didn't stop me from worrying about my family.

"Does this mean you've made your decision?" Erebus asked.

"Yes." I stood straighter, thinking about Blake. He needed us. The *world* needed us to take back Medusa's head. We might be running away from a battle… but it was so we could win the war. "We're ready to continue on our journey."

CHAPTER FIFTEEN

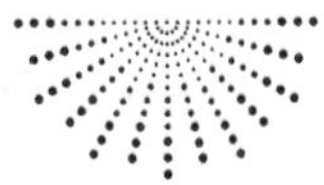

We continued walking along the path, past the portal, until reaching the forest. The footprints of the giants were pressed into the dirt, and I placed my foot inside one, curious about how it would size up. The giant's foot was triple the size of mine.

If we'd been walking along the path minutes earlier, we would have come head to head with the giants, who would have likely crushed us in their sprint for the portal. We'd been lucky this time. But I knew better than to think that the luck would continue. When facing the next monster, would we just run away like we had when coming across the Nemean lion? I tightened my grip on my bow, feeling like a coward as I remembered how we'd turned and ran. We'd been relying on our powers since the night of the comet—

the thought of fighting without them was terrifying. Hopefully Apollo's gifts would help us through whatever battles were to come.

Erebus stopped at the forest. I stopped behind him, craning my neck to look up at the towering trees. Their trunks were wider than a car, and I tried to see to the top of them, but I couldn't. They grew up into the clouds. For all I knew, they were as tall as the mountain itself.

Tendrils of fog reached out from the forest, as if beckoning us to enter so it could wrap itself around us and never let us go. Despite the stifling heat, goose bumps rose along my arms. Every instinct in my body warned me to back away and run in the opposite direction.

"Are you sure this is the best way for us to go?" I asked Erebus, taking a step back. "The forest seems kind of…" I paused, searching for the right word. "Scary" and "creepy" came to mind first, but they weren't strong enough to get across my feelings.

"Ominous," Danielle finished the sentence for me.

"Yeah." I nodded. "Exactly. And we already know the giants were in there… what if there's something worse inside?"

"You're right to be afraid of the Whispering Forest," Erebus said. "But the path through the forest is the *only* path that will take you up the mountain, besides the direct route that you already tried. And we all know how that ended up, so I trust you won't be trying that again. But I assure you—there's nothing in that forest that will harm you. Physically, at least."

"But it'll harm us in other ways?" Chris asked.

"It can," Erebus said. "Once you've entered the forest, it's easy to get lost inside. Many do. Some creatures wander in the mist for years, or centuries. When —or *if*—they emerge, they're never the same. The forest breaks their minds."

I shivered, not liking how that sounded.

"Luckily, the three of you have me as your guide," he continued. "It's about a three-hour walk from here to the other side of the forest, and we'll hold hands and make a chain as we walk to make sure that no one gets lost. During that time, you must remember—the wind will whisper through the trees, preying on your fears, but none of it is real. No matter what, you *must* remember that."

"Got it." Chris nodded. "Is there anything else we should know?"

"You won't be able to see or hear each other in the forest," Erebus said. "So whatever happens, hold onto each other's hands, and don't let go."

"And if something happens, and we do get separated?" I asked. "How will we find each other if we can't hear or see each other?"

"That won't happen," he said.

"But if it does?" I pressed. "What then?"

"Then you have two options. Get lost in the forest, or get ahold of yourself and follow the path to the exit. As long as you remember that nothing you hear is real, you shouldn't get separated at all. But if you *do* get separated, then for your sake—and for the sake of everyone living on Earth—I hope you're strong enough to remain on the path. Because once you wander off the path, you'll be nearly impossible to find. And if you're lost, we do not have the time to spare to go back for you. Understand?"

"Yes," I said, somber with the weight of his words. "I understand."

I looked back into the forest, the fog so thick that it was like a ghost calling to me. Beckoning to me. What was it going to *say* to me? What was so horrible that it could drive even the most dangerous monsters crazy for centuries?

Fear crept up my spine, but I straightened, pushing it away. No matter what happened, I couldn't trust anything I heard in there.

Blake was counting on me. The *world* was counting on me. And I refused to let them down.

CHAPTER SIXTEEN

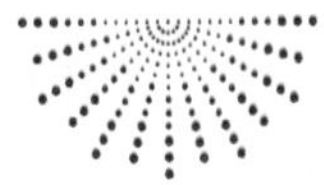

"I'll be the caboose," Chris volunteered, glancing at Erebus. "Since you'll be in front, I figure we've gotta protect the girls."

"You are no less vulnerable than they are," Erebus said. "But as you wish." He reached for Danielle's hand, and soon the four of us were linked together—Erebus leading the way, then Danielle, then me, and Chris in the back. We were all sweaty because of the heat, but Chris's palm was much more slippery than Danielle's. I guessed that despite his attempt to sound brave, he was just as scared as I was. But it would embarrass him if I mentioned it, so I said nothing.

Erebus took his first steps into the forest, and we had no choice but to follow him into the mist. The first tendril of fog licked my fingers, and I was surprised by how silky and cool it was—a welcome break from the smothering heat. I made my way fully into it, contentment seeping into my skin as it covered me completely.

My insect bites, which had itched so much that they'd burned—cooled down in the fog until the burning was gone. It was as if the bites had never existed at all. My hunger and thirst were gone as well. The fog was thinner near the ground, so I could see my feet and the path. Above that, I couldn't see more than a few inches around myself. But I didn't care. This was the most comfortable I'd been since coming through that portal.

Perhaps this was why creatures entered the forest and never returned—they realized how comfortable it was here, and they made a choice. As the peaceful calm rolled over me, it wasn't hard to understand why they had no desire to leave.

"Why did you say this was going to be hard?" I asked Erebus. "The three hours we'll be in this forest will probably be the best ones in Kerberos. Besides the moment I see Blake again, of course." I smiled, thinking of our upcoming reunion. I couldn't wait to run into his arms and kiss him again, and finally tell him that I loved him.

No one answered my question, and I opened my mouth to repeat myself when I remembered—we wouldn't be able to hear each other in the forest. Erebus never told us *why*, but I guessed it had something to do with the fog.

Not being able to see anything or talk to anyone for three hours was going to get boring pretty quickly, but a little bit of boredom wasn't something to complain about compared to everything else we'd seen in Kerberos so far. At least wasps weren't trying to sting us and beasts weren't trying to kill us.

We continued walking for what felt like an hour, although in the fog, it was hard to tell how much time had passed. Then a breeze rustled through the leaves. It was soft at first, but it got louder and louder, like whispers whistling in the wind. The whispers were all around me, but I couldn't hear what they were saying.

I squeezed Chris and Danielle's hands, relieved when they squeezed back. I might not be able to talk to them, but I understood the message they were trying to get across—they heard the whispers, too. But we had each other. We would be fine.

As we continued, the whispers got louder. I couldn't hear what they were saying, but they were like insects, crawling into my ears and lodging themselves into the crevices of my brain. They filled my head, whistling and hissing until my mind felt like it might explode from the force of it all. I wanted to let go of Chris and Danielle's hands and lodge my fingers into my ears to dig out the voices.

But I didn't. I held on tighter. Erebus had warned us that nothing we heard in the forest would be real. The whispers weren't *actually* in my head. They were figments of my imagination.

Unfortunately, simply acknowledging that they weren't real didn't make them go away. They just got louder and louder, until each little whispering voice surrounded me, closing in on me until I couldn't hear my own thoughts above their hissing.

"Shut up!" I yelled into the fog. My friends might not be able to hear me, but maybe whatever lurked in this forest could. "Get out of my head!"

I didn't think the whispers would listen to me.

But they stopped, as if someone had hit the power button to shut them off, and all was silent.

CHAPTER SEVENTEEN

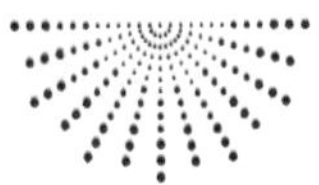

"Nicole?" a familiar voice asked, barely louder than a whisper. "Is that you?"

"Becca?" I stopped walking, searching for where her voice could be coming from. But Danielle pulled me along, forcing me to continue.

I remembered what Erebus had said earlier—*whatever you hear in there, it isn't real.* The voice I just heard might sound like Becca, but it wasn't her. It was the forest playing tricks on me.

"Nicole?" my sister asked again, her voice trembling. "Where are you going? Don't leave me here. Please."

I pressed my lips together and continued on, saying nothing. Whatever this thing was that was pretending to be my sister, I refused to play its game.

But even though I didn't respond, it kept talking.

Repeating my name, asking where I was, begging me to come and find her.

To find it, I reminded myself. This thing wasn't Becca. Becca was back in Kinsley, safe in our house. There was no way that she was here. She *couldn't* be here.

But even though I said nothing, that didn't stop it from talking.

"Why are you ignoring me?" she asked, and given her tone, I could imagine Becca's pouty expression when she said it. "I know that you're special now since you have those powers, but you're still my sister. Why won't you come help me? Do I mean nothing to you now, since I'm not special like you are? Don't you love me anymore?"

"You're not my sister!" I yelled, unable to stay silent for a second longer. My breaths were heavy, but I steadied myself, trying to regain control. All I wanted was for this *thing* to stop talking to me. "I don't know what you are, but you're not Becca."

"You're wrong," she whispered.

"I'm not wrong."

"Are you really going to leave me here?" she asked. "Lost, in this forest? I'm scared, and I'm cold, and I want to go home. Don't you want to help me?"

"You're trying to trick me." I gritted my teeth

together, determined to make this creature shut up. "I know better than to fall for it."

"What if I told you something that only I would know?"

I said nothing. Because this thing *wasn't* my sister. And nothing it said would make me believe otherwise.

"Remember that time a few years ago, when I broke Mom's teapot in the dining room?" she said, even though I hadn't asked her to continue. "I felt so bad about it—I couldn't stop crying. But you cleaned it up and threw it in the neighbor's trashcan. You said Mom would never notice. And you were right—she didn't notice, until we were packing up to move to Kinsley. She asked what happened to that teapot, and we both acted like we had no idea what she was talking about. We were so calm about it—until we ran into your room, shut the door, and burst out laughing."

I couldn't help smiling at the memory. Becca and I didn't have much in common, but we did occasionally have moments that brought us together. We still shared a smile whenever we walked by the replacement teapot in our dining room now. We were the only ones who knew what had happened to the original—and since we'd promised to never tell anyone about it, we were the only ones who would *ever* know.

So how was she telling me this story now? Was I right to have worried that my family might have left the safety of the house? Did one of the creatures from Kerberos find Becca and force her through the portal?

She'd been kidnapped before—it could happen again. Had she been brought to Kerberos and dropped into the forest?

"A monster captured me and brought me here," Becca continued, as if she could read my mind. "I was terrified, but I remembered when the other monster brought me to the cave, and how you saved me. You'll save me again, Nicole, won't you? You won't leave me here alone?"

I looked around as Danielle pulled me forward, searching for where Becca's voice was coming from. All I could see was the white fog. Surrounding me. Blinding me.

"Where are you?" I called into the forest. Maybe I could get the others to come with me to find Becca. Once we got out of here with her and I explained to them what happened, they would understand that I had no choice—I *had* to save her. "Tell me where you are."

"I don't know." She whimpered. "It's foggy, and I'm scared. Come find me. Please. I'll die in here if you don't."

She sounded so frightened and helpless. I knew we should have gone after the giants and killed them to make sure our families were safe. If I'd stood my ground more, we would have done that. Once the giants were taken care of and we knew everyone was safe, we could have come back to Kerberos to continue our mission.

Instead, I'd been weak. It was my fault that Becca had been kidnapped. I had to find her. Yes, our mission was important, but I refused to abandon my family.

I tugged on Danielle, trying to get her to stop walking. But she gripped my hand tighter, pulling me forward.

I couldn't let her continue. I didn't know where Becca was, but she was *here* somewhere. If we kept walking, we would lose her. So I yanked on Danielle's hand again, harder this time, determined to make her stop.

Instead of listening to me and stopping, she curled her thumb inward and dug her nail into my palm—deep enough to draw blood. I screamed and tried to wrench my hand out of hers, but then I stopped struggling.

Because with the pain came a sudden clarity.

This thing in my head wasn't Becca. If Becca were close enough to talk to me—to *whisper* to me—she would have run to me and found me herself.

I held Danielle's hand tighter, hoping to communicate to her that she got through to me, and continued walking forward. I took a deep breath, centering myself. I had to stay focused. I'd let the whispers invade my mind once—I refused to let them do it again.

"Nicole?" the voice asked, softer this time. "Aren't you coming to find me?"

"You're in my head!" I yelled into the void. "I don't know what you are, but you're not Becca. You might be able to access my memories, but I won't fall for your tricks. What we're doing is too important. Blake's counting on me. My family's counting on me. The *world* is counting on me. And I won't let them down."

The whispers could say whatever they wanted, but they couldn't hurt me. And so, feeling more confident than I had since first stepping into the forest, I relaxed and kept walking.

Then Chris suddenly slipped his hand out of mine, and he was gone.

CHAPTER EIGHTEEN

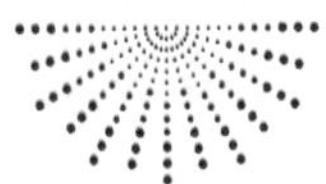

I reached for Chris, but he was nowhere to be found. And Danielle continued to pull me forward, unaware of what had just happened.

I couldn't leave Chris out there. So I did the first thing that crossed my mind—I used my free hand to jab Danielle below her ribcage. The instant she lost her breath, I pulled my hand out of hers and turned around, screaming Chris's name. Of course he couldn't hear me, so I held both my arms out and ran back from where we'd come, hoping to bump into him. It had only been seconds—he couldn't have gone far.

I stayed on the path, since if I left it, I might never find my way back. Hopefully he'd stayed on it, too.

If he hadn't, he could be lost forever.

"Nicole?" another whisper entered my mind.

"Blake?" I asked, even though I knew it wasn't actually him. He was no more real than Becca.

"Who else?" I could practically hear the smirk in his tone.

"But I saw the dragons fly you up the mountain." I wasn't sure if I said it more for his benefit, or for mine—to remind myself that this wasn't really Blake.

"Yeah, they did," he said. "And I've gotta say—being flown by dragons was pretty cool. We need to try it sometime. But don't you know me well enough by now to know that I could fight off Ethan on my own? I was coming back down the mountain to find you—that's how I got here—but it looks like you found me first."

I wished it were true so badly that it hurt. I was cold, and alone, and scared. This mission would be so much easier if I had Blake by my side. I wanted him to be here, and I had no doubt that the forest knew that, too. That's why I was hearing him now.

But I refused to stop looking for Chris. The fog, the whispers, the forest—I didn't know what kind of creature this was, or what kind of magic it had, but it could somehow get into my mind. It wanted to keep me here. And to do that, it had to separate me from my friends.

Technically, it had already succeeded.

But I refused to give up hope. I would find Chris, and get out of here. And maybe—just maybe—I could use the forest's desires to my advantage.

"Blake," I said, wanting to hear his voice again. "I missed you."

"You have no idea how much I missed you." Despite the cold, hearing him speak made warmth rush through my veins. "I fought off Ethan and ran through this hell world to find you. *That's* how much I love you, Nicole. Enough to run through hell for you. I love you more than you could ever know."

"You love me?" My voice cracked, and a tear rolled down my cheek.

"Of course," he said. "And since you entered hell for me, I don't think I'm going out on too much of a limb to think that you love me, too."

"Yes." I tried to wave the fog away, needing to find him. But I had no idea where his voice was coming from. It was everywhere and nowhere all at once. "Of course I love you. I've loved you since Greece, and I was so terrified that I would never get a chance to tell you."

"You don't need to worry anymore," he said. "Because I'm with you now, Nicole."

"Where?" I asked, my heart leaping into my throat. "I'm trying to find you, but I'm lost and I can barely see. Tell me where to go."

"Turn right, and keep walking straight," he said. "We'll be together soon, Nicole. I promise."

Every molecule in my body wanted to turn right and run into Blake's arms. Instead, I jabbed my thumbnail into my palm, digging into the exact same spot Danielle had cut into earlier. A fresh wave of pain shot through my arm, cleansing my mind of the hypnotizing whispers.

Before they could take hold of me again, I turned left, and I ran.

CHAPTER NINETEEN

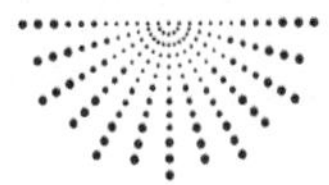

I crashed into Chris a few seconds later.

"Chris!" I exclaimed, even though he couldn't hear me. Knowing I had to work fast, I reached for his shoulder and dug my nails into the place where the fox had scratched him.

His chest vibrated with the force of his scream. Seconds later, he was still. But at least he wasn't fighting me, which must have meant that the pain shocked him out of the hypnosis caused by the whispers.

I reached for his hand, ready to guide him back to the path. But he grabbed my hand and turned it over, tracing something onto my palm. Letters. First a T, and then a Y.

Thank you.

I did the same, tracing a Y onto his palm, and then a W.

You're welcome.

I linked my hand into his, holding tightly this time. I wouldn't let us separate again. I'd tricked the whispers once, but now they knew to expect it from me. I wouldn't be able to trick them again. All I could do was make sure Chris and I stayed on the path, and that we kept walking until we reached the end of the forest.

As we continued, I heard my mom, my dad, Kate, and even Apollo. All of them trying to convince me that they were here, and that I needed to come find them. But I kept my fist clenched as I walked, digging my nails into my flesh to remain focused.

Finally, the path ended. I stepped out of the fog, Chris emerging after me.

"Nicole! Chris!" Danielle ran up to us, wrapping her arms around us and pulling us into a big hug. "I knew you would make it out of there. Erebus said you wouldn't, but I told him he was wrong and forced him to wait with me." She pulled out of the hug and stepped back, studying both of us. "What *happened* back there?" she asked me. "You were trying to break away from me, and I pinched you to bring you back to focus. I thought it worked, but then you *punched* me and ran off."

"Sorry about that," I said. "Chris broke away from

me, and you weren't letting me go, so it was the first thing I could think to do to break free."

"And you found him that easily?" Erebus asked. I wasn't sure when he'd approached us, but his arms were crossed, and he watched us with interest.

"Yeah," I said, and I quickly explained how I'd let myself believe the whispers, only to pinch myself to remind myself to go against them at the last minute. "I figured that since they could get in my head, the only way to make them trust me was to make myself believe what they were telling me."

"Smart." Erebus nodded. "I didn't expect that from you. It must have taken a lot of willpower to break away from the delusion on your own. Good job."

I wasn't sure whether to take that as an insult or a compliment, so I said nothing. Instead, I turned back to Danielle. "How did you know to pinch me to force me to get back into focus?" I asked her.

"I tried to break away from Erebus at one point, and that's how he brought me back," she said. "It worked on me, so I figured it would work on you, too."

"You couldn't have told us about that *before* we entered the forest?" I asked Erebus.

"I'm only your guide," he reminded us. "I was hoping you would figure it out for yourselves. But when Danielle tried getting away from me, I did it without thinking. Once it was done, I couldn't take it back."

"Don't sound *too* happy about saving my life," Danielle said, rolling her eyes. "And the lives of Nicole and Chris, since they wouldn't have known to do that if it hadn't been for you doing it to me first."

"What's done is done," Erebus said. "The important thing is that we made it through the forest without losing anyone."

"Yeah," I said, not wanting to think about what would have happened if I hadn't found Chris—or if I'd ended up stuck in that fog, too. How long would I have wandered around aimlessly, talking with my loved ones and searching for them even though they weren't anywhere to be found?

I wanted to ask Chris what he'd heard that made him run away, but I stopped myself. Because what we'd each heard was personal. I wasn't ready to share my experiences with them, and it wouldn't be right to push them to share theirs with me. At least not so soon after it happened.

So I said nothing, instead remembering what it had felt like to hear Blake's voice—to hear him say that he loved me. It wasn't real, but I wanted it to be. I wanted it so badly that it hurt.

The others were quiet as well. Were they also remembering what they'd heard in the forest?

"Do you all need to rest?" Erebus asked, breaking

the silence. "As a god, it's easy to forget that humans need to sleep sometimes."

"No," I said, since hearing Blake's voice had brought about a new wave of energy to find him.

Danielle and Chris said they were able to keep going as well.

"Good," Erebus said, turning to continue on the path. "Because the Whispering Forest was just the beginning. We have a lot of ground to cover before reaching the mountain."

CHAPTER TWENTY

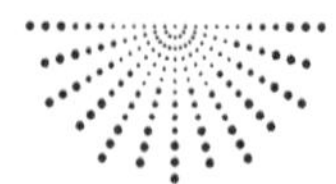

We didn't have long to walk until reaching our next destination—a river. The moment the path curved and we saw the water, I sprinted to the edge, cupped the water in my hands, and took a long drink. Chris knelt beside me, doing the same thing.

The water was sweet and delicious—like it had come straight from a glacier itself. It was better than any water I'd had on Earth. Which surprised me—because wasn't this a *prison* world? It didn't seem very prison-like to have such delicious water. But it was here, and I was thirsty, so I wasn't going to complain.

I drank and drank until I couldn't fit any more in my stomach, and then I sat back, using my sleeve to wipe the water from my chin.

"This water's amazing," Chris said, finishing up a

handful and diving in for another. "If we bottled it up and sold it on Earth, we could make *millions*."

"If only we didn't have to seal the portal," I joked, feeling much better now that I didn't feel like I was going to pass out from thirst. I turned around, wondering why Danielle wasn't joining us, surprised to see her walking slowly toward us with Erebus. "Aren't you thirsty?" I asked her. "This water's amazing."

She pressed her lips together and glanced at Erebus. When she turned back to me, she looked like she wanted to tell me something, but like she didn't know how to start.

Before I could open my mouth to ask her what was wrong, dizziness slammed into my head, my vision hazed over, and everything went dark.

CHAPTER TWENTY-ONE

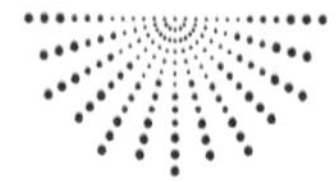

I woke up in the cave, staring straight into the glowing yellow eyes of the harpy. My hands rested on the back of a chair where Becca was seated, her wrists and ankles binding her down.

"The choice is yours," the harpy said, its eyes on me. "If you refuse to hand over the Book, the energy of six witches will make my friends in there very happy." It pointed a talon at the muddy door—the portal to Kerberos—and cackled.

I blinked a few times, centering myself. I remembered this happening—back in January, the week when we first got our powers.

How did I get here? What was happening? The last thing I remembered, I was drinking water from a river in Kerberos.

What had the water *done* to me? Had it sent me back in time?

Danielle stepped forward and stuck her chin in the air. "What's to stop you from throwing us in there even if Nicole gives you the Book?" she asked.

I looked at her, trying to see if she noticed anything was off. But she simply stared at the harpy, waiting for it to answer. The others did the same—including Kate. She stood to the back, near the cave wall, and I gasped at the sight of her. I didn't think I would ever see her again. I *hoped* we would be able to break Medusa's curse, but who knew how long that would take—*if* we were even able to succeed. But here she was, as if nothing had ever happened to her.

Maybe *that* was the reason why I was here. To save Kate.

"Just my word," the harpy answered Danielle's question and smiled to the best of its ability, given that it had a beak instead of a mouth.

"Because that's *so* reliable." Becca sneered.

The harpy raised a talon and slashed it across Becca's face, blood spritzing all around her. I gasped, my heart sinking into my stomach. Because that wasn't supposed to happen. But Becca's screams made it clear that it *had* happened, and she hunched over, her agonizing wails echoing through the cave.

I ran around the chair, placing my hands under

Becca's chin and forcing her to look up at me. The moment I did, I wished I hadn't. The harpy's claw had slashed diagonally across my sister's face, along one of her eyes, slicing her nose in half and deforming one side of her mouth. Her eyeball had *popped*, the gooey remains of it dripping down her cheek.

My beautiful sister looked like a monster.

"It'll be okay," I told her, barely able to find my voice. "I can fix this."

I reached forward to heal her, but before I could, the harpy pushed me to the side. I crashed to the ground, my breath knocked out of me. Before I could process what was happening, the harpy picked up Becca's chair and threw it across the room, sending it hurtling over the nearby cliff. My sister's screams echoed through the air. I heard a crash, and she was silent.

"No!" I screamed, running to the side of the cliff. I looked down, collapsing into sobs at the sight below. Becca's head had crashed into a stalagmite. Her skull was crushed to a pulp, her remaining eye staring emptily up at the ceiling.

The sight of her broken body chilled me to the bone. A minute ago she was fine. Now she was gone.

I would never be able to see my sister or talk to her again.

How was this happening? I remembered this day—this wasn't how this was supposed to end. Becca was supposed to be fine. She couldn't be dead. She just *couldn't* be.

But there she was, crushed to death at the bottom of a pit. And there was nothing I could do to save her.

Something grabbed my arm—the harpy's claw—and she forced me around to face her. "Don't be too sad about your sister," she snarled. "Because you'll be seeing her soon."

She reached her other claw forward and dug it into my chest. I screamed—the pain so unbearable that I couldn't think or move or breathe.

She pulled her hand out of my chest, I saw my bloody heart dripping in her claw, and everything went dark.

CHAPTER TWENTY-TWO

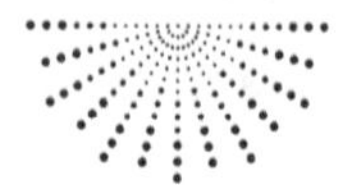

When I opened my eyes, I was back on the yacht in Greece, holding what was left of Chef's arm after he'd been mauled by Scylla.

He glanced down at what was left of his arm and scowled. "You're supposed to be a *healer*," he said, yanking the remaining stump back to his side. "What good are you if you can't fix this?"

"What's happening to me?" My chest burned with pain, but when I looked down at it, it was fine—no hole where my heart should have been. "Why am I *here*?"

"What's happening to *you*?" Chef asked, his features twisted in rage. "Are you crazy, girl? You're the one who was supposed to fix what happened to *me*!" He waved his stump in the air, glaring at me as if I'd ripped his arm off myself.

Blake wrapped his arms around me, and I sank into his embrace and closed my eyes, sobs wracking through my body. At least Blake was back here with me. That was one comfort in this huge mess.

"She saved your *life*," Blake said to Chef, his chest vibrating as he spoke. "If Nicole wasn't here, you would have bled out and died."

"Stop talking, boy," Chef said, and then Blake choked, a heart-dropping gurgling sound coming from his throat as he gasped for air.

Warm liquid dripped down my cheek, and Blake's body went limp around me, collapsing to the ground. His blood was everywhere—in my eyes, on my face, in my hair, on my hands. It poured out of his neck, from the gash that Chef had sliced through his throat.

I reached for him to heal him, but Chef dropped his knife and pulled me back, his arm wrapped around me so tightly that he crushed my ribcage.

"No!" I screamed, thrashing against Chef's hold. "Let me go! You have to let me heal him!" I kicked and screamed, but he was stronger than me. I was trapped, watching helplessly as the life drained out of Blake's eyes.

His fingers twitched a few times, and he was still.

"Blake," I said, tears streaming down my face when I said his name. He couldn't be dead. He had to hold on. I couldn't lose him, too.

How was I supposed to go on when I was losing everyone I loved?

"I could have healed him!" I yelled, still trying to fight Chef's iron grip. "Why didn't you let me heal him?!"

"You wanted me to let you heal your boyfriend, when you couldn't even heal me?" His hot voice flooded into my ear. "Not a chance. You're worthless, girl. And worthless things don't belong on this boat."

He threw me to the ground, picked up the bloody knife, and the point of it was the last thing I saw before it slammed through my skull.

CHAPTER TWENTY-THREE

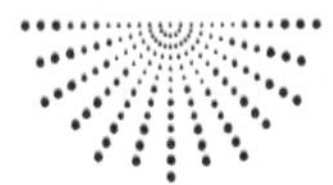

When I opened my eyes next, I was in the Hydra's cave, staring at Rachael's swollen, blackened body.

"No." I pulled my hand off her arm, not wanting to touch her. "Not here. I don't want to be here. I can't take any more of this. Please—make it stop." My head pounded in the spot above the bridge of my nose—where Chef had stabbed me—and I rubbed it, trying to make the pain go away.

"What are you talking about?" someone asked from next to me—Ethan. He stared at me, his eyes crazed and hollow. "Can you save my sister?"

I stared back at him, saying nothing. I'd already gone through this once. I couldn't do it again. I couldn't tell him that I'd failed. That I was the reason why his sister was gone.

"I'll take your silence as a no." He raised something above his head—the Hydra's fang, dripping with tar-like poison—and rammed it through my heart.

I struggled for one last gasping breath, and then Ethan smiled wickedly, twisted the fang, and everything went dark.

CHAPTER TWENTY-FOUR

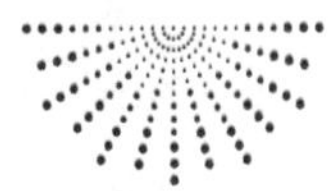

This time when I opened my eyes, I was running down my street in Kinsley. My heart burned where Ethan had stabbed it with the Hydra's fang, but all I could think was—*keep running. You have to get home.*

This was different from the other times. Those times, I'd woken up during something that had happened to me in the past. Where I was now—running down my street, trying to get home—wasn't something from my past. This felt real.

Then again, the first few times I'd woken up had felt real, too. For all I knew, they *were* real now.

Could reality as I knew it have been changed?

No, I thought. Because that would mean that Becca was dead, and Blake was dead, and that *I* was dead.

Which I clearly wasn't, because here I was, running down my street in Kinsley.

Had something happened to me in Kerberos? Something that made me black out, have gruesome visions, and wake up having no idea what I'd done between then and now?

I had no idea. All I knew was the one thought repeating in my mind—I had to get home.

Everything in Kinsley looked exactly how it had been when I'd left, down to the muddy snow in piles along the sides of the street. Finally I reached my house, and I ran up to the porch, swinging the door open and hurrying inside.

A dismembered arm waited for me in the entranceway, flung onto the floor like discarded trash. The silver watch on the wrist was unmistakably my step-dad's. The man who had raised me—who felt more like my dad than Apollo himself.

I keeled over and threw up. Once my stomach had emptied, I ran through the living room, screaming for my parents. People could live without arms—Chef had lost an arm, and he'd survived.

Just because I'd seen my dad's arm didn't mean he was dead.

But then I entered the kitchen, where more limbs dangled from the ceiling. My dad's other arm, both of my mom's arms, and both of their legs. Hanging with rope, dripping blood into puddles on the tile floor.

I screamed, falling onto my knees at the sight of the morbid scene before me. This couldn't be happening. Hadn't there been a protection spell around the house to keep monsters from entering? How could one of them have gotten through? This couldn't be real.

I shut my eyes, trying to make it all disappear. But when I opened them again, nothing had changed. My kitchen was a slaughterhouse.

I had to get out of here.

I ran back to the living room, and that was when I saw them—two heads, placed on the coffee table like decorative ornaments.

My mom and my dad.

I screamed again and collapsed on the floor in heaving sobs, covering my eyes as I cried. My parents were gone. I couldn't think, I couldn't move—all I could feel was the bone-chilling realization that I would never be able to see them again. How was I supposed to live through this? It wasn't fair. Why was I alive, and they were dead?

More importantly—who did this to them? And *why*?

Then someone opened the door, and it slowly creaked open until hitting the wall. I looked up, and saw a figure in a black cloak standing in the doorway, his features covered in shadow.

He pulled out a gun and aimed it at my head.

The bang of the shot threw me back into the darkness.

CHAPTER TWENTY-FIVE

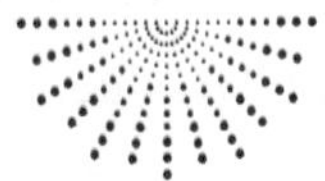

I woke up to a thunderous crack and gasped for air. The horrible scenes I'd just lived through flashed through my mind—images of all the people I loved, dead. My heart raced, the chill of loss pounding into my bones as my eyes fluttered open.

I was lying down in the center of a small boat. It was the size of a fishing boat, but made of all wood. Erebus and Danielle stared down at me, both of them sitting on a bench at the back. Danielle casually drank from a bottle of water, and Erebus manned the oars.

"What just happened?" I pushed myself up to a sitting position and rubbed my temples, trying to force the images I'd seen out of my mind. I glanced next to me, where Chris was still asleep, his blank expression showing nothing of whatever he was experiencing in his mind. Hopefully it wasn't anything as horrible as what I'd gone through just now.

Now that I was awake, it was clear that all of those terrifying, gory scenes had been dreams. But they'd felt so *real* when they were happening. I'd never been prone to nightmares… was *that* what they were like?

I shuddered, trying to shake the horrors away. I would never laugh at my sister again the next time she woke up screaming and scared from a dream.

"You drank from the River of Dreams." Erebus unzipped his bag and pulled out a full water bottle, tossing it to me. "I wish you'd told me you were thirsty," he said. "I would have offered that to you if I'd known. And those are automatically refillable, by the way. They'll never go empty."

He *should* have offered us water upfront instead of letting us assume he had some in his bag, but I didn't want to complain to a primordial deity. So I opened the bottle and took a swig. The water wasn't as delicious as the water from the River of Dreams, but it would do.

"That river's seriously called the River of *Dreams*?" I asked, shaking my head. "It was more like the River of *Nightmares*."

"The water from the river makes whoever drinks it pass out and have vivid nightmares of their worst fears," Erebus explained. "All the fresh water in Kerberos comes from the river. Immortals don't need food and water to survive, but we do experience hunger and thirst, although at much greater intervals than mortals. Those locked in Kerberos have a choice—deHydrate themselves to an unbearable level of thirst, or drink from the River of Dreams and descend into their worst nightmares. Both options are agonizing, and are enough to drive anyone mad, especially after centuries of torture."

I nodded as I took in his words, grateful that he'd brought us water bottles so we wouldn't have to make that same choice. Although after those nightmares, I had no doubt that I would deHydrate myself forever if it meant never seeing those horrible visions again.

"How long was I asleep?" I asked. Dark gray clouds still covered the sun, so it was impossible to tell what time it was. "And where are my bow and arrows?"

"About four hours," he said. "I got you and Chris onto the boat, and we've been floating down the river ever since. I stored your weapons inside the bench while you were asleep." He stood up, opened the bench, and handed me my bow and quiver. I swung both of them over my back, feeling complete now that I had them back on me.

"Will Chris be up soon?" I glanced at his sleeping body again.

"He had more water than you, so he'll be asleep for

longer," Erebus answered, situating himself back down. "He should wake up relatively soon, though."

"Good," I said, and then I glanced at Danielle, who had just taken another sip of her water. "How'd you know not to drink from the river?" I asked her. "I know you knew. I saw the guilt in your eyes when I asked you why you weren't having anything to drink, right before I fell asleep."

"Erebus told me," she said. "At first, I wanted to run to the river with you and Chris. But he pulled me back and told me to stop. When I asked him why, he told me, but it was too late to stop you and Chris—you'd already started drinking the water."

"You were all running fast, and I only had time to get to one of you," Erebus added. "Danielle was closest."

"It would have been a lot easier if you'd warned us about the water *before* we were running distance from the river," I said.

"And I would have thought that you knew better than to run up to a river in a *prison dimension designed to torture those inside of it* and start drinking from it," he said, his eyes sharp.

"I was thirsty," I said, although heat rose to my cheeks and I glanced down at my feet, since I knew he was right.

He sat back and shook his head. "You should just be glad that it was a shallow part of the river, and not a part where any creatures live," he said. "If they'd sensed you, they would have pulled you under before you knew what was happening."

I shuddered, not wanting to think about the what-ifs. I'd already had enough torture for one day.

"Do you want to know another reason why Danielle was the one I stopped?" Erebus asked, continuing before I could answer. "Because despite being thirsty, she was the only one who paused to think about what she was doing."

"I got the message the first time you said it," I said, glaring at him. "What I did was stupid and impulsive, because I should have known better than to trust anything in Kerberos. And after the nightmares I just had from that water, you can sure as hell trust that I won't make that same mistake again. So there's no need to rub it in anymore. Okay?"

"I wasn't rubbing it in," he said. "I was just ensuring that my point got through. You were *lucky* that the only thing that happened to you was a few bad dreams. If you'd done something else—for instance, if you grabbed one of those fruits hanging from the trees overhead—it would be a whole lot worse."

"What happens to people who eat the fruit?" I looked up, noticing them for the first time. They resembled peaches, except they almost seemed to *glimmer*. My mouth watered at the sight of them.

"You don't want to know." He leaned back and rowed faster, making it clear that he wasn't going to say any more.

"Fine," I said. "But since we're on the topic of food, and you told us to let you know when we need anything, I guess I should tell you that I'm starving."

"Now you're getting the hang of this." He paused his rowing again to open his backpack and pull out a protein bar. "I've got enough in there for the entire trip, so whenever you're hungry, let me know."

I devoured the protein bar, and was soon onto my second. Mid-way through eating it, Chris jolted up, his face twisted in horror. He scrambled to the side of the boat and retched over the edge.

"Where am I?" he asked once he'd gotten control of himself. "What just happened?"

Erebus told him exactly what he'd explained to me after I woke up. Chris relaxed as he listened, apparently glad that what he'd just experienced had only been in his mind.

I wondered what he'd seen, but I didn't ask because of the same reason that I hadn't asked after the forest—our experiences had been so personal. I didn't want to *think* about my nightmares, let alone tell them to someone else.

Once Erebus finished his explanation, he handed Chris two protein bars, apparently figuring that Chris would be just as hungry as I was. Chris thanked him, and we all sat in silence as we ate, looking around as the boat floated down the river. Tree branches canopied above us, shielding us from the amber, overcast light that I'd come to associate with Kerberos, and making it possible to imagine that I was still on Earth.

For the first time since arriving here, it actually felt peaceful.

Until something whacked into the side of our boat with enough force to send us toppling to the floor.

CHAPTER TWENTY-SIX

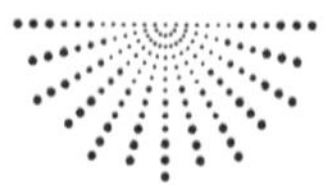

"What was that?" I peered over the edge of the boat, trying to see what we'd crashed into. Something whammed into the opposite side, and if I hadn't been holding on to the edge, I would have gone flying into the water.

"Merpeople," Erebus muttered, at the same time as the boat got another whack. It rocked back and forth, as if caught in a storm, and we all held on tight to make sure we didn't go flying over the edge. He rowed faster, but it made no difference—the boat wasn't moving.

A slimy, webbed hand reached over the edge, gripping onto mine with a surprising amount of strength.

I reached into my quiver for the arrow I'd used on the fox and jammed it into the hand. It lost its grip, and it and the arrow flopped back into the water. Now that I was free, I pulled away and removed my knife from my boot, hurrying to the center of the boat. I held up the knife, ready to stab any merpeople who tried to attack.

"Get to the center!" I yelled to the others. "Quickly!"

They did as I said, and we huddled in a circle in the center, holding onto each other to keep steady. Chris and I each had our knives out, and Danielle had her sword.

Webbed hands gripped at the sides, and then the merpeople surfaced. With hair like seaweed, bulbous faces, bulging eyes, and gaping mouths, they were nothing like the beautiful mermaids I used to imagine existing as a kid. They were creatures from nightmares, and they hissed and screeched at us, showing us their rows of sharp teeth and reaching forward with their slimy hands to try to pull us into the river.

"Only their top halves can go above the surface—their tails have to stay in the water," Erebus said. "And whatever happens, don't let them pull you in. They won't try to take a bite out of you while you're still alive, but drowned mortals are their favorite food."

More and more of them surfaced, rocking the boat harder and harder. If we capsized, that was it. We would drown before we were able to fight them.

So we would have to fight them from here. Since they were in close range, I shot one of them with my other used arrow, the shot going straight through its chest. The mer-creature gasped and sunk back into the river. I'd hoped that seeing that would scare the others away, but instead they screeched louder, apparently angered even more. Danielle swung the Golden Sword at the ones she could reach. The dismembered arms fell into the boat, but more of them were surfacing by the second, making her fighting futile. And I couldn't use my three remaining arrows now. There were too many of them and not enough of us. Plus, if I used all my arrows now, I knew I would regret it later.

"Chris!" I yelled at him. "You need your lyre!"

"It's in the bench," Erebus told us, and I groaned, because there was no way to get to the bench while avoiding the merpeoples grasps. Chris must have realized that too, because he stared at the bench, his eyes wide with horror.

"You have no idea how much I miss my power right now," he muttered. "With the wind on our tail, we could blow away from here in seconds."

"Well, you don't have your power," Danielle stated the obvious. "So we have to do this another way. You get that lyre—I'll fight off any merpeople that try to stop you with my sword."

They hurried toward the bench, and Danielle swung

at any arms that reached out to them. Chris opened the bench and pulled out his lyre—but just as he did, a hand reached out from behind Danielle, grabbing her non-sword arm and pulling her and her sword down into the river.

CHAPTER TWENTY-SEVEN

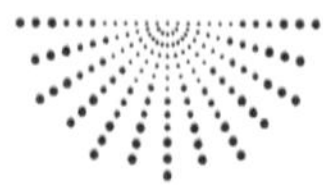

I pulled out a crystal arrow and ran to the side of the boat, ready to shoot the merperson who'd taken Danielle. But the water was so dark that I couldn't see anything beneath the surface. I wanted to dive in after her, but I had no way of fighting those creatures in the water. Jumping in would be suicide.

Then there was a splash behind me. I looked to see what had happened, and saw Erebus's pack on the ground. The spot where he'd been standing was empty.

He'd jumped in after Danielle.

Another merperson reached for me, but just as it did, Chris started playing his lyre.

"Stop attacking us," he commanded, his voice fluid with the melody of the music. "Swim as far away from us as possible and forget that you ever saw us."

The merpeople stopped rocking the boat and descended back down into the water. For the first time since they'd started attacking, all was still.

I leaned over, trying to see what was happening with Danielle, but the water was too dark for me to tell.

"Where's Erebus?" Chris asked, apparently only just noticing that he was gone. "He didn't get pulled in too, did he?"

"He jumped in after Danielle," I told him.

"Good." Chris sighed. "Then Danielle will be okay. Those creatures won't stand a chance against a god."

Seconds later, Erebus surfaced with Danielle by his side. She coughed and took a deep breath, her eyes panicked as she looked around. "They're gone?" she sputtered, taking in the scene. "You got the lyre?"

"Yep." Chris smiled and raised it up. Then he held out a hand to help Danielle onto the boat.

She tumbled back on board, still gripping the Golden Sword. At least, despite everything, she'd had the sense to not let it go.

I held out a hand to help up Erebus, but he scowled at me and climbed up easily on his own. Once they were both back on board, Danielle squeezed her hair, attempting to comb out the remaining seaweed. Which was strange, because back on Earth where Danielle had her powers, she was able to dry herself off immediately. Now, as she sat there rubbing the water out of her eyes, she seemed so small and weak.

Instead of having control over her element, it had control over her.

"Did you swallow any of the water?" I asked her, wanting to be prepared in case she was about to fall into a nightmare-filled sleep.

"Nope." She shook her head and shivered, staring at the river. "That was terrifying," she said. "I've gotten so used to being able to control water. It's my element, but here, it could have killed me. If Erebus hadn't jumped in to save me, it *would* have killed me."

"Is that your way of saying thank you?" he asked.

"You saved my life, so I don't think 'thank you' is strong enough to get across what I'm feeling right now," she said. "But yes. Although… and I don't want to sound ungrateful, because I'm not—I thought you weren't supposed to interfere with our journey? You're just supposed to be our guide?"

"I saw you and the sword go under, and my instinct was to jump." He shrugged and sat back down with the oars to start rowing. "That sword's been in legends for thousands of years. It would be a shame to have such a glorious weapon lost in the bottom of a river in Kerberos."

"So you jumped in to save the sword." Danielle eyed him up, as if making sure she was hearing this correctly. "And while you were at it, you decided it wouldn't hurt to save me, too?"

"Something like that," he said, rowing faster. "Are you disappointed? If so, I can throw you back in and you can see how you fare with the merpeople on your own."

"No!" She scooted closer to the center of the boat, pulled her legs up to her chest, and wrapped her arms around them. "I don't ever want to go in there again."

"I didn't think so," he said. "And just so you know—I wouldn't actually throw you back in there. I might only be your guide, but I *do* want to keep the three of you alive."

"That would be easier if we weren't floating along a river full of monsters," I said. "Nothing else is going to burst out of the water and try to drown us, right?"

"That wouldn't have happened if it hadn't been for Chris's… reaction to his nightmares," Erebus said. "The creatures in the water don't notice the boat. It's made of wood, so it's part of nature. But the moment Chris vomited into the water, they were clued in that we were here. So as long as you keep all parts of yourself *inside* the boat for the rest of the trip, we'll be fine."

"I didn't know," Chris defended himself. "I thought I was doing you all a favor by aiming out of the boat."

"We know," I told him. "We don't blame you."

I wanted to ask *what* he'd seen in his nightmares that

caused such an extreme physical reaction when he woke up, but I held back. After all, the last thing I wanted to do right now was to think more about my nightmares by talking about them, and I assumed he felt the same. So we floated along in silence for a few minutes, looking around and taking in our surroundings. It was peaceful again, but I knew better than to think that would last.

"How much longer will we be on the river?" Danielle eventually asked. "And where's it taking us?"

"We're traveling to the other side of the mountain," Erebus answered. "It should take a few hours. The path that we'll be taking starts there, and it's only accessible from the river. The journey up that path will be exhausting, so even though time is limited, I recommend you get some rest now."

I shouldn't have been tired, since I'd just woken up. But the nightmares had hardly been restful, and after I lay down, it didn't take long until the boat rocked me to sleep.

CHAPTER TWENTY-EIGHT

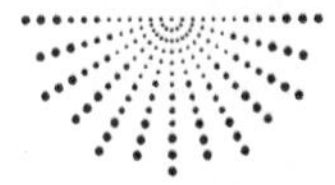

I woke up shivering. I sat up, since it was too cold to sleep, and found Danielle already awake. She huddled in Erebus's sweatshirt, rubbing her hands over her arms to try warming up. Chris was still sleeping, although by the way he kept stirring, I had a feeling it wouldn't be long until the cold woke him up, too.

I walked over to join Danielle and Erebus, hoping that being near the edge of the boat would block some of the wind. "How long was I asleep?" I whispered, not wanting to wake up Chris.

"About four hours," Erebus answered.

"Did you sleep at all?" I asked him. "I could take over rowing if you want to get some rest."

"I'm a god," he reminded me. "I don't need sleep."

"Oh." I sat back, my teeth chattering from the cold. "That must be nice."

"It is and it isn't," he said. "Sometimes I find myself jealous of the way mortals can 'check out' from the world for a while. Us gods don't have that luxury."

"I would like to not need sleep," Danielle chimed in. "Imagine how much you could get done with all that extra time—everything you could learn and accomplish. It would be incredible."

"I have no doubt that you would be a fierce goddess." Erebus looked out at the river, appearing to be deep in thought. "But you must remember that time has a different meaning to gods than to mortals. Mortals get so much done in their short lives because they're constantly worried about running *out* of time. When time is endless, it's easy to lose that zeal. Everything can get put off, until you realize that a century has gone by and you've accomplished nothing of any importance. I think that's part of why I'm helping the three of you now. When I look back on the past few centuries, they're as empty as the darkness I personify. Nyx pointed that out to me when she asked me to help you, and she was right. I've given into indifference for far too long. It was about time that I do something—even something as strange as leading three mortals through a deadly hell dimension and ensuring that they return safely to Earth."

"You're helping us save the world," Danielle said, placing her hand over his. "Without you, we wouldn't have made it this far. We owe you our lives. Everyone in the *world* owes you their lives."

"We haven't reached the end yet," he reminded us. "There are still many challenges ahead."

We sat in silence for a few seconds, and I rubbed my hands over my arms, trying to get warm. "I don't suppose you have another sweatshirt in that bag?" I asked Erebus, still keeping my voice down so I didn't wake Chris.

"Nope," he said. "But I can give you my shirt if it'll help." He stopped rowing and lifted his shirt above his head. His body was absolutely perfect—which wasn't surprising, since he was a god.

Even though I loved Blake, it was impossible to resist checking Erebus out. Not doing so would be like being in front of one of the most beautiful pieces of art in the world and not stopping to admire its beauty.

Danielle's eyes were on Erebus too, her cheeks red. She quickly pulled her gaze away from him and focused on the floor. But he smirked at her as he handed me his shirt—apparently he'd noticed her checking him out, too.

"Thanks." I took the shirt from him, wrapping it around my shoulders like a shawl. It did help guard me against the wind, and I stopped shivering as much. "I guess gods don't get cold, either?"

"We feel the cold, but it doesn't bother us like it does a mortal," he said. "Extreme temperatures are uncomfortable, but they can't kill us. And since I'm your guide, it makes sense for me to sacrifice some personal comfort if it can help save your lives."

The line of what Erebus could and couldn't do to help us seemed to be getting blurrier as he spent more time with us, but I said nothing. It was kind of him to help—and it didn't seem wise to irritate a god who was on our side.

"Maybe once Chris wakes up he'll need your pants," Danielle joked, although from the way her eyes roamed down Erebus's body, I had a feeling that if that were the case, she wouldn't complain.

"I heard that," Chris mumbled from where he was curled up into a shivering ball. "And I might be cold, but I'd rather Erebus leave his pants *on*." He sat up and stretched, raising his arms above his head. But then he winced, and he grabbed his shoulder, right where the fox had scratched him when we first tried going up the mountain.

"Since we have some time, you should let us have a look at that shoulder." I tried to be casual about it, since Chris didn't want us making a big deal about his injury.

But the pain I'd seen on his face concerned me. If I could help, I had to try.

"It's fine." Chris sat straighter and forced a smile. "It's just a scratch."

"I'm sure it is," I said. "But we have time right now, and even scratches need to be cleaned. Just let me have a look, okay?"

"You're acting like you're a doctor." Chris laughed.

"I may not be a doctor, but I liked to run around a *lot* outside when I was younger," I told him. "I got scraped up constantly. I know how to clean up something like this. It's not a big deal—it'll just take a minute."

"She's also a daughter of Apollo," Erebus chimed in. "Healing's in her blood."

"Fine," Chris said. "It doesn't hurt that bad, but you can have a look."

He pulled his sleeve up, and I scooted over to him to check out the injury. The scratch wasn't huge, but the skin around it was red and puffy. I knew before touching it that it would be warm. Sure enough, it was.

"You don't have any medical equipment in that bag, do you?" I asked Erebus. "Some antibiotic ointment, or antibiotics themselves?"

"No," Erebus said. "And if the fox bit him, it wouldn't help, anyway. They have a poison in their saliva that can't be treated by any medicines on Earth."

"The fox *scratched* him," I clarified, turning to Chris so he could back me up. "Right?"

"The fox *gave* me a scratch on my shoulder." Chris lowered his eyes, refusing to look at me. "But it wasn't with his claws. It was with his teeth."

"Well, this is just great." Danielle sighed and pulled Erebus's sweatshirt tighter around her. "What are we supposed to do now? We know nothing about this poison. How long does it take to set in? What are its effects?"

"For immortals, the poison causes torture and pain," Erebus told us. "In mortals, it brings on a slow, painful death. It can take weeks—sometimes even months—to take full effect."

"That's good," I said, relief setting into my chest.

"Maybe I missed something, but can you explain to me how that's *good*?" Chris asked.

"We won't be in Kerberos for much longer," I reminded him. "A day or two at the most, hopefully. Then we'll go back to Earth, and once we're there I can use my power to heal you. You'll be fine." I looked back at Erebus so he could confirm it.

He said nothing, his eyes dark.

"What?" I asked him. "Is there something you're not telling us?"

"It's nothing." He waved off my question, but the darkness didn't leave his eyes.

I didn't feel like dealing with the God of Darkness being broody right now. So instead I poured some water from my bottle onto the sleeve of the shirt he'd given me and used it to clean the scratch on Chris's shoulder.

"How does that feel?" I asked him. I didn't know if it would work, but I hoped it would at least cool it off, or maybe even remove some of the poison.

"A little better," he said, giving me a small smile. "Thanks."

"Do you think the pain will affect your fighting?" I asked him. "And be honest with me. It's no good trying to be manly and brave about it if it'll just put you in danger."

"It's my right shoulder, and it feels stiff, so it might affect my fighting a bit," he admitted, rolling it around a few times. "But I can still use my lyre."

"We have to remember what Apollo said about the lyre," I reminded him. "Every time you use it, it'll go more and more out of tune, until the magic is gone completely. We have no idea how many times you'll be able to use it before that happens. So we need to save it for when we're up against more creatures than we can possibly fight on our own—like what just happened with the merpeople. If it's only one or two —or even three—creatures, then Danielle has her sword and I have my arrows. We also all have our knives. We should use those weapons *before* you use the lyre."

"How many arrows do you have left?" Danielle asked.

"Three—all of them still unused," I answered. "And I know to be careful with how I use them."

"Good." Danielle nodded. "So, here's how I think we should go about this. Since the Golden Sword works as long as I have it, the first priority should always be to use the sword. If I need backup, fight with your knives if you can. If we're far away and the creature doesn't look like the type we can win against in close-up combat, *then* use an arrow. The lyre is only for if we're so overwhelmed by enemies that we have no other choice." She looked at Chris, and then at me, her eyes full of determination. "Got it?"

"Yes," I said, and Chris echoed my sentiment. "Got it."

CHAPTER TWENTY-NINE

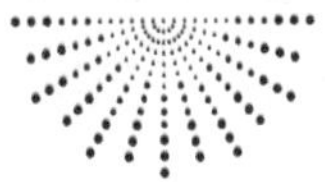

An hour later, Erebus docked the boat at the start of an open, winding path. Out in the distance was the mountain—looking much farther away than it had when we'd first come to Kerberos through the portal.

"This is where we get off?" I asked, trying to figure out how far we were from the mountain. It was impossible to tell.

"Yes," he said, and the moment he spoke, thunder echoed overhead. Suddenly, the sky was pouring down buckets of rain—so thick that it obscured the view of the mountain. But the rain wasn't above our heads. It started at the bank of the river. Once we exited the boat, we would have no choice but to step into it, as if passing through a curtain.

I stuck my hand out to feel the temperature of the rain. It was so cold that I gasped and pulled my hand back.

"How are we supposed to walk through that without getting hypothermia?" I asked Erebus. "It's *freezing.*"

"You might be mortals, but the three of you have the blood of the gods running through your veins," he reminded us. "You can withstand far more extreme situations than humans. Think about Antarctica, when you were coming back from Chione's ice palace. You rode through negative forty-degree weather without proper attire and still managed to make it to the South Pole station alive. No human could have done that."

"We were *barely* alive," I reminded him. "If I wasn't able to heal myself and the others, we probably would have died."

"If you were human, your death would have happened before you were able to use your power at all," Erebus said. "Yes, the hike to the mountain will be uncomfortable, but as long as you remain focused on the purpose of this mission, it will not kill you. Now, as promised, I'll lead the way."

He dropped his oars and stepped out into the rain. The three of us followed him. The rain poured down, so cold that it felt like ice on my skin. But we had to get through this.

And so, I gathered my focus, remembering what Erebus had said about the blood of the gods giving us strength, and forced myself forward.

CHAPTER THIRTY

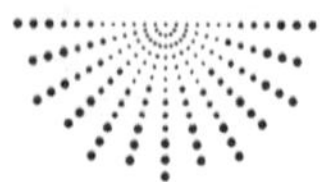

I wasn't sure how long we walked through the storm. It felt like hours, and since it was one long plain, there were no places to stop to take cover. We had no option but to trek on.

It wasn't close to as cold as in Antarctica, but the rain was so icy that I suspected it was nearly freezing outside. My body hurt from shivering so much, and every step felt heavy. I assumed that making us uncomfortable, but not to the level where it killed us, was on purpose—it wouldn't be much fun to torture creatures in a hell dimension if those creatures died.

My time here so far had taught me that the worst type of torture *wasn't* the type that killed you. It was the type that barely allowed you to go on alive, so that you could live and be conscious through the anguish and the pain.

We continued along the path, saying nothing. Not like I *could* speak given how much I was shivering. I was soaked to the bone—if we ever made it out of this rain, I doubted I would ever feel dry again. All that kept me going were thoughts of my family at home counting on me, and of Blake up at the top of that mountain needing our help. Without that drive, I surely would have collapsed and succumbed to the cold by now.

Then, when I was seriously contemplating falling into a heap on the ground and curling up into a ball until the rain stopped, the downpour lightened.

"I don't want to speak too soon," Chris said, his teeth chattering. "But does it seem like the rain is letting up?"

"Yes." Danielle looked ahead, and she brightened. "Out there." She pointed. "Look. It's not raining."

As we'd been walking, I'd been keeping my eyes on my feet—it helped me focus on the task of putting one foot in front of the other. But when I looked forward, I saw what Danielle was pointing at. The base of the mountain was within sight, and right ahead of it, the rain came to a sudden stop.

Filled with a newfound vigor, I bolted into a run, eager to escape the rain. Danielle and Chris ran as well. Erebus turned into a shadow and disappeared—I assumed he'd had enough of the rain and was going to meet us at the place where it stopped.

I was right—when we reached the end of the rain, Erebus was waiting in front of a looming gate at the start of the mountain. He was dry, which wasn't fair, but it was miraculously warmer here, so I couldn't complain.

"If you can travel by shadow, why'd you stay in human form when we were walking through the rain?" Danielle asked him.

"I thought it would boost morale if I endured the journey with you." He shrugged. "It was less comfortable, but I knew I would survive."

"And you knew we would survive too, right?" Chris asked. "Since we have the blood of the gods in our veins?"

"I was pretty sure of it."

He sounded more sure than that before we'd started off, but I ignored him for now, instead enjoying my time in the sun. This was the first place we'd been in Kerberos where the sun shined through the clouds. The sun here was dimmer than the one on Earth, more of a dark amber than a bright white-yellow, but it warmed my skin just the same. I held my face up and closed my eyes, relishing its rays. After those hours of trekking through freezing cold rain, it felt amazing to take a few seconds to breathe and take in the light.

For the first time since arriving in Kerberos, things finally felt like they were looking up.

"Umm, you guys?" Chris asked, the panic in his voice breaking through my thoughts. "What's that?"

I opened my eyes and saw three bird-humanoid creatures—harpies—flying through the air and heading straight toward us.

CHAPTER THIRTY-ONE

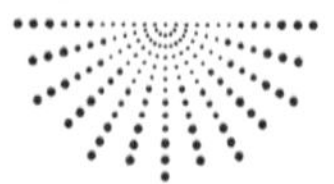

"Watch out!" Danielle screamed, unsheathing her sword and readying herself to fight. I did the same with my bow, although I hoped I wouldn't have to use any arrows, since I only had three left.

But the harpies didn't attack. Instead, they landed a few feet ahead of us, their yellow eyes studying us suspiciously. I kept an arrow strung, warning them not to come closer, but didn't shoot. Danielle and Chris kept their weapons raised as well.

"You come from Earth," the harpy in the center finally said. "Descendants of the gods." She looked at me specifically, observing the Golden Bow. "Judging from Apollo's weapon in your hand, you're the Daughter of Apollo—the one attempting to re-seal the portal between Earth and this hellish prison world."

"How do you know who I am?" I asked, keeping my arrow aimed straight at her heart. I couldn't miss, and she must have known that too, or she probably would have attacked by now.

"The Titan goddess Phoebe prophesied your existence centuries ago." The harpy smiled as much as she could through her beak. "She said, 'led by Nyx, the Daughter of Apollo will ignite elemental powers in four other descendants of gods, and with the guidance received from the Book of Shadows, the five of them will work together to seal the portal to Kerberos.'"

"You've known about me all this time?" I was so shocked that I couldn't move. But it explained why so many monsters had attacked me after they'd escaped Kerberos. They wanted to stop the prophecy from coming true.

"It was infuriating to be trapped in this place, unable to interfere," she said. "But of *course* we knew about you. How else would my sister have known to search you out after she escaped?"

I swallowed, barely able to breathe. The harpy I'd killed in the cave—the one who had kidnapped Becca and I'd killed using black energy—was this creature's *sister*.

There was no way this confrontation could end without a fight.

"You met her," the harpy observed. I hesitated, and

she added, "Don't try denying it. I can see it in your eyes. And I wouldn't recommend shooting me either." She eyed my arrow, not looking scared in the slightest. "I can see from looking at your quiver that you only have three crystal arrows left. And you haven't even started up the mountain yet! Using them now would be a grave mistake, don't you think?"

She was right, but I didn't want to admit it. So I held my ground and said nothing. She wouldn't dare step any closer if she thought there was a chance I would shoot.

"My sister was determined to destroy you," the harpy continued, apparently taking my silence as agreement. "She said it wouldn't take long, and that once the job was finished, she would come back to retrieve us and we would escape into Earth together. We waited, and waited... but she never came back." She sized me up, her gaze glinting with suspicion. "All I ask of you, young demigod, is to tell us what happened to her. Once you do, we'll let you through the gates."

"I recommend you listen," one of the other harpies said from behind her. "Without us letting you through, the only way to open those gates is if we're dead."

"I thought this was supposed to be the *easy* way up the mountain," Danielle muttered, glaring at Erebus. He, of course, smirked and said nothing. So she turned away from him and re-focused on the harpies, her sword poised and ready to kill.

"You want to know what happened to your sister?" I asked the harpy, leveling my gaze with hers and putting as much confidence into my voice as I could manage. "I killed her. Just like I'm about to do to you."

With that, I pulled back on the string of my bow and shot the crystal arrow straight through her heart.

CHAPTER THIRTY-TWO

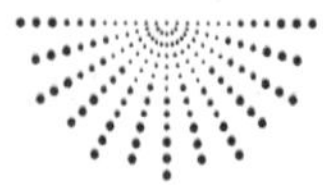

The arrow killed her instantly. I don't even think she had time to realize what had happened. She toppled to the ground, and dust billowed out around her, so thick that it hid her body.

The other two harpies squawked and ran toward me. Their eyes flashed with anger, and their wings expanded, giving them more speed. Danielle sprinted toward one of them, swinging her sword in a perfect arc that chopped the harpy's head clean off. But the other harpy was moments away from running into me. I didn't have time to reach for my knife, so I grabbed another arrow, strung it onto my bow, and shot it through her heart.

She toppled to the ground in front of me, and all was still.

"So... that went well." I took a few steps forward so I was standing over the harpy. Her back was toward the sky, and the arrow hadn't come through—it must have lodged itself in her heart.

I leaned down to roll her over, but she was nearly three times my size, so heavy that she didn't budge.

"I could use some help over here!" I called over my shoulder.

Chris ran over and positioned himself over the harpy. When I'd asked for help I was hoping that Erebus would come, but he'd walked to the gate and was running his fingers over the metal. Danielle stood over the harpy she'd killed, using its feathers to clean her sword.

"Are you sure you're up for this?" I asked Chris. "I'm sure one of the others can help."

"I have a *scratch*," he said. "I'm not an invalid. At least not yet."

We worked together to roll over the harpy, maneuvering her so she was on her back. Her eyes stared up at the sky, the shock of her final moment plastered across her face.

The arrow stuck straight out of her chest, and I pulled it out, studying the dulled crystal. It was covered in blood. Following Danielle's idea, I used the harpy's feathers to clean it off. Once it was as clean as it was going to get, I stood back up and placed it into my quiver, catching sight of Chris massaging his shoulder. His eyes met with mine, and he lowered his hand.

"Are you sure you're okay?" I asked him.

"I'm fine," he assured me, flexing his hand at his side. "Come on. Let's get the other arrow."

The first harpy—the sister of the one I'd killed in the cave—had landed on her side. The arrow stuck out into the air. We didn't have to turn her over, but Chris hurried ahead of me and placed his foot on her stomach to hold her still, yanking the arrow out of her chest. He used his left hand—not his dominant one, since his right shoulder was the one that had been injured.

I didn't know what he was trying to prove, but I said nothing, since the task was already done.

He rubbed the arrow on his jeans to clean off the excess blood and walked over to me, placing it into my hand. "Use these next time," he said, his eyes serious. "You only have one active arrow left. You have to save it for when you really need it."

"I know," I said. "But that harpy was going to kill me if I didn't kill her on the first shot. I *had* to use one of the crystal arrows."

"What about the first harpy?" he asked. "Did you have to use one of the active arrows on her, too?"

"I didn't want to miss."

"You're a daughter of Apollo," he reminded me. "You don't miss."

"That's not entirely true," I said. "I missed when we were fighting Medusa."

"How could I forget?" He smirked. "You got me straight in the other shoulder. But that doesn't count. Because in case you don't remember, Ethan spiked our drinks with gray energy that night. *All* of our powers were off."

"Which is exactly my point," I said. "Our powers were off then, just like they are here in Kerberos. None of us can access our elemental powers. Why should my ability to shoot be any different?"

"Because your power to shoot isn't an *elemental* power," he said. "It's inherited. You shoot like you do because you're Apollo's daughter. Being in Kerberos can't take that away from you."

"Maybe." I shoved the used arrow into my quiver, since looking at it reminded me that I only had one active arrow left. "But I didn't want to test it out when my life was on the line."

"So let's test it out now," he said.

"Are you serious?" I asked, even though I could tell from his impish smile that he was. "What would I even shoot? There aren't any trees around here to use for target practice."

"Hey, Erebus!" Chris yelled to the god, who was still over at the fence, deep in discussion with Danielle. "Come over here for a second!"

Annoyance crossed over his face, but he disappeared into a cloudy shadow, reappearing next to us a few seconds later. "You called?" he said, his tone dripping with sarcasm.

"I need your help with something," Chris said. "What would happen if you were shot with one of the used arrows?"

He glanced up at the sky, contemplating the question. "It would hurt for a second," he said. "Then I would remove the arrow, heal, and pulverize whoever had the nerve to shoot me."

"Stop being ridiculous," I said to Chris. "I'm not going to shoot Erebus."

Danielle arrived at our side, needing more time than Erebus to get there since she actually had to use her legs. "What are you talking about?" she asked me. "Why would you *shoot* Erebus?"

"Relax," I told her, unable to stop myself from laughing. "I'm not shooting anyone."

"But you need to shoot *something*," Chris said, and then he turned to them to explain. "Nicole's avoiding shooting the used arrows because she's afraid she's gonna miss."

"I'm not *afraid*." I placed my hands on my hips and glared at him. "I'm being cautious."

"Because you're afraid that being in Kerberos made you lose your ability to shoot along with your ability to heal." He stood straighter and crossed his arms over his chest, not backing down.

"Fine." I grabbed a used arrow from my quiver and slid the bow off my back. "What should I shoot?"

Erebus reached for the dead harpy at our feet, grabbed her wing, and pulled her up to a standing position as if she weighed nothing. "Aim for the same spot you shot her last time," he instructed, holding onto the monster so she didn't fall down. "Her heart. I doubt your aim will be so terrible that you'll miss and shoot me instead. If it is, then at least you know I won't die. *And* I promise I won't pulverize you."

"Well, at least there's that," I said, spinning and walking away to give myself room to shoot.

"Although I can't promise that I won't tell Apollo!" Erebus added. "I'd hate to think what *he'd* do if he found out that a child of his missed her target *that* badly."

"It won't be an issue." I positioned myself fifty feet away from the harpy and strung the arrow onto my bow. "Because I won't miss."

I steadied my bow and eyed up the red dot on the harpy's chest where the arrow had pierced her skin the first time. Erebus watched me, an annoyingly arrogant smirk on his face. I didn't know if he was smirking because he thought I was going to miss, or because he was confident I could do this.

I had to prove the latter. Because he was right—it *would* be humiliating if I missed.

And so, zeroing in on the target, I pulled back on the string and sent the arrow flying toward the harpy.

CHAPTER THIRTY-THREE

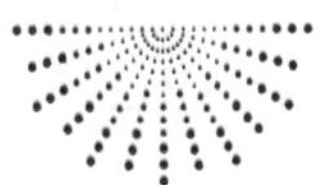

"Bullseye!" Erebus announced, dropping his hold on the harpy and letting her crash back onto the ground.

I jogged back over to where they were all standing, leaning forward to inspect the shot. "That's not a bullseye," I said, yanking the arrow out of the harpy's chest. "If it were a bullseye, there would still only be one hole. But there's not. There are two."

"Seriously?" Danielle rolled her eyes. "They're like, an inch apart, and you were fifty feet away. Seems like a bullseye to me."

"It was a good shot," I agreed. "But not a bullseye."

"You children of Apollo are so picky," Erebus said. "I told you to aim for the heart. Your arrow hit the heart. Thus… a bullseye."

"At least you know you haven't lost your ability to shoot," Chris said. "So save that last active arrow for an impossible shot, all right?"

"I will," I promised, adding the used arrow back into my quiver. With only three arrows left—and only one of them active—I would have to be careful to use the two used arrows only in situations where it would be possible for me to retrieve them.

"Now that that's finished, you both need to hear what Erebus and I were discussing by the gate," Danielle said, turning her attention to the god. "Do you want to tell them, or should I?"

"You go ahead," Erebus said. "Since it was your idea to ask in the first place."

"Okay." Danielle flipped her hair over her shoulder, and I had a feeling that she'd planned on being the one to tell us even *before* she'd asked Erebus. "First let me explain how I got to asking the question in the first place. You see, when anyone dies on Earth, they go to Hades—the underworld of Earth. So after the harpies died, I wondered… what happens when creatures die in *Kerberos*? Does Kerberos have an underworld of its own?"

"It's a good question," I said, and then I turned to Erebus. "Do creatures killed here even *go* anywhere? Or are they just gone forever?"

"No creature—mortal or immortal—is ever 'gone

forever,'" Erebus said. "The physical form may perish, but the soul is everlasting, and cannot be destroyed. And Danielle is correct that Kerberos has its own version of the underworld—a dark, miserable place where the soul takes no form. It floats alone in the shadows for all eternity, conscious and aware that it's powerless to escape."

"What happens to the creatures who die here who don't deserve a place like that?" I asked. "Is there somewhere else they can go? Someplace more similar to Heaven?"

"Kerberos was created by the original primordial deity—Chaos—to imprison the most dangerous creatures on Earth," he explained. "In the Second Rebellion, we—the primordial deities—knew that if the Titans won, there would be no future for this planet. And so, Nyx filled a comet with her magic and sent it soaring across the sky, opening the portal to Kerberos and gifting the Olympians with enough power to force all those who rebelled against them inside. Then, once the comet disappeared, the portal sealed. We hoped it would remain sealed forever. But as you know, that's not what happened."

"Clearly," Danielle said. "Do you even know how we're supposed to seal the portal? Because I know we need to seal it, but we still haven't been told *how* to do that."

"You'll find out in time," he said. "But I deviated from your original question. The short answer is—every creature in Kerberos is here for a reason. Once killed here, they have no opportunity for a pleasant afterlife because they do not deserve one."

"What if one of *us* dies in Kerberos?" Chris asked. "We're not prisoners here. Would we get sent to the underworld here, too?"

Erebus gazed up at the mountain and took a deep breath. "When Chaos created Kerberos, I don't believe he took it into consideration that *any* creature would enter this world by choice," he finally said. "It's never been done before."

"What about those born in Kerberos?" I asked. "Like the Cyclops who escaped through the portal. Why should he be punished when he couldn't have even been alive during the Second Rebellion?"

"I assure you—he *was* alive in the Second Rebellion," Erebus said. "When in Kerberos, no creature is able to age or procreate. Most of the Cyclopes actually supported the Olympians in the Rebellion. But there are extremists in all groups, and as such, there was a small sub-sect of Cyclopes who supported the Titans. The Cyclops who escaped was part of the sect. Do not be deceived by his age—Cyclopes age slower than humans. Though he appeared young, he was actually older than you are. If Ethan hadn't used Medusa's head on him, he was most likely planning on doing something equally bad, if not worse, to you once you had him in that cave."

"At least I don't feel guilty anymore about having him turned to stone," I said, remembering how I'd hesitated before Ethan had brought out the head.

"Ethan was correct in what he did," Erebus agreed.

I nodded, remembering the Cyclops's final scream as he turned to stone. Which of course reminded me of Kate's final scream, which made my heart hurt for my lost friend. I wanted to believe that her final moment wasn't painful, but given the agony in her scream, it was impossible to convince myself that that was true.

"So we *have* to make sure we stay alive while we're in Kerberos," Chris said, bringing me back into focus. "Not that I was planning on anything else, but we can't, under any circumstances, end up in the underworld here."

I shivered, not wanting to think about the consequences if that were to happen. At least on Earth I knew that when I died, I would be reunited with my loved ones in the afterlife. Not even having *that* to comfort me was unimaginable.

"The possibility of ending up in the underworld here scares me, too," Danielle said, her voice surprisingly soft. Then she stood straighter and rested her hand on the grip of her sword, her eyes strong with determination. "So we can't let it happen. We have to get up that mountain, get the head, stop Ethan, and then all of us—Blake included—have to get out of here as fast as possible. Because the sooner we're back to Earth, the safer we'll be."

"So let's keep going," I said, turning toward the mountain. Blake was up there, and we were going to find him. I refused to settle for anything less. "We have no time to waste."

CHAPTER THIRTY-FOUR

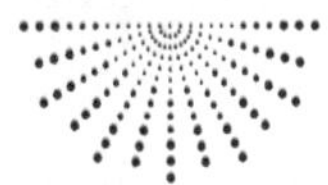

Erebus opened the gate, and we all walked through, starting up the winding path that ascended the mountain. Surprisingly, nothing jumped into our way to try to kill us, and the temperature was neither too hot nor too cold. A slight breeze blew against my skin, cooling off the places where I'd been bitten and stung by the wasps.

I didn't want to say anything, because I was sure that once I did *something* would jump out at us and prove me wrong, but this area was actually pretty nice. I could only assume that after the Badlands, the Whispering Forest, the River of Dreams, the merpeople who tried to drown and devour us, the freezing rain that nearly wore us to exhaustion, and the harpies who'd wanted us dead, that most people didn't make it this far. So the mountain didn't need to set up any torture traps.

If we didn't have Erebus as our guide, I doubted we would have made it this far, either.

"Is it just me, or is this place too good to be true?" Chris asked, also looking around as if waiting for something to attack.

"This area of Kerberos is deceptive," Erebus warned us. "We have to keep moving, and we can't stop until we reach the point where the grass is dead."

"What happens if we stop?" I didn't plan on stopping, since we needed to get up the mountain as quickly as possible, but still, I was curious.

"A lightning bolt will strike you down and cause you more pain than ever imaginable."

"Oh." I glanced up at the amber sky. "Good to know." There were a few wispy clouds, but nothing that looked like it could create lightning. Still, I picked up the pace, just to be safe.

We walked for about three hours, making sure to keep moving. Finally, the grass ended abruptly and turned to dirt, forming a clear line along the land. I stepped over the line, taking a moment to uncap my water and take a sip.

Then the wind blew from up ahead, and I smelled something strange—something metallic and rusty.

"Do you all smell that?" I asked, sniffing the air some more.

"Yeah," Chris said. "It smells like… death."

"Not death." I shuddered at the idea of whatever we were approaching. "It smells like *blood*." The wind stopped blowing, so the smell wasn't coming at us anymore, but the remains of the scent lingered in my nose. It was definitely blood.

Danielle stopped walking and eyed up Erebus. "I'm guessing you know what's ahead," she said. "So if you want to warn us, now would be a good time."

"We're approaching the Red River." He faced the breeze and took a deep breath, not reacting to the smell at all. "Crossing will be difficult, but I trust that you will figure out how to do so successfully."

"Why will it be difficult?" I pressed.

"That's up to you to discover yourselves." He continued forward without bothering to look back at us.

With nowhere else to go, and since we clearly weren't about to get an actual answer, we followed his lead.

The smell grew stronger, until I could taste the blood in the back of my throat. The air was hot and sticky, and when we turned a corner I saw it—a river of bubbling blood. It was like the blood was boiling, evaporating into the air. But that wasn't the strangest part.

Because around the river were horses… although they weren't like any horses I'd ever seen.

Their *bottom* halves were horses, but their necks morphed into the top halves of humans.

"Centaurs," Danielle breathed.

The moment she spoke, one of their heads twisted in our direction. He caught sight of us and smiled.

"Humans," he said, and before I knew what was happening, all of the centaurs galloped toward us, forming a circle around us so we couldn't escape.

I readied myself to grab my knife from my boot, although it wouldn't be much of a defense against the centaurs. There must have been thirty of them in all. They licked their lips, digging their front hooves into the ground.

The four of us clustered together in the center of the circle, tensed and prepared to fight.

The centaur that spotted us walked toward us, staring down at us as if we were bugs he wanted to squash. "Not humans," he said, taking a few deep sniffs of the air around us. "I smell magic in your blood."

"We don't want any trouble," Danielle said, although she reached for the handle of her sword and wrapped her fingers around it. "We just need to cross the river."

"Cross the river?" The centaur laughed, and the others laughed along with him. "Why do you wish to cross the river?"

"Our friend was taken to the top of the mountain," I said, pointing up at where the peak of the mountain disappeared into the clouds. "We need to get up there so we can help him escape."

I purposefully left out information about Medusa's head—since these creatures were locked *in* Kerberos, I doubted they would support our mission to seal the portal. The last thing we needed was to give them a reason to want to kill us on the spot.

"That's unfortunate," the centaur said. "If your friend was taken to the top of the mountain, he's surely already dead." He paced around in front of us, eyeing us suspiciously. "Where did you say you were from again?" he asked.

We didn't say where we were from, but he knew that, so I said nothing. Neither did Danielle and Chris.

"It's no matter." He waved away the question. "Because do you know what we do to anyone who trespasses on our land?"

"No," Chris said, meeting the centaur's gaze without flinching. "But I have a feeling you're about to tell us."

The centaur stopped pacing, and he stared at us. "The first thing we do is kill them," he said simply. "Then we slash their necks and hold them upside down over the edge of the river so their blood can drain into the water. Once their body is empty of blood, we feast on the parts that remain. Bones and all." He smiled, showing off his sharp teeth.

"Is that it?" Chris asked, not looking scared in the slightest.

"What's your problem?" The centaur sneered at him. "Do you want to die, boy?"

"Not particularly."

The centaur's eyes glinted with amusement. "Then this isn't your lucky day, is it?"

"Actually, I think it is." Chris smiled and reached for the Golden Lyre, starting to play. Each note rang clearly through the air, filling a massive amount of space for such a small instrument.

All of the centaurs were suddenly still, their eyes glazed over as they listened to the music.

"None of you are going to kill us," Chris continued, his voice melodic and hypnotizing. "You're going to take us across the river, and once we're gone, you'll return here and forget you ever met us."

The centaur who had previously threatened to kill us nodded, his face slack. "Our biggest men will jump you across the river," he agreed. "Once we've brought you to safety and you're out of our sight, we'll return here and forget we ever met you."

"That's what I'm talking about." Chris stopped playing the lyre and swung it around his back. "Kneel down, horsey," he said to the centaur. "Because you're my ride."

CHAPTER THIRTY-FIVE

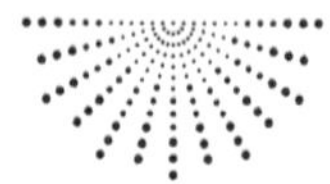

We each hopped on a centaur, and I held on tight to its mane as the creature ran toward the river, gaining speed before he jumped. We soared through the air, landing smoothly on the other side. They let us off their backs, and once we'd dismounted, they turned away, as if they'd forgotten our existence.

We ran over the crest of the hill, wanting to get as far away from them as possible.

"Nice job," Danielle told Chris once the Red River had disappeared behind us. "I was about to tell you to use the lyre, but you pulled it out before I could."

"There were too many of them and not enough of us," Chris said, reaching for his injured shoulder and massaging it. "The lyre seemed like the safest bet."

"Since we're out of the lightning zone, do you want

to stop so I can check your cut?" I asked him. "It could probably use a cleaning after all that walking."

"I'm fine." He dropped his hand back to his side. "I was just holding onto the centaur too tightly. It's not bothering me anymore."

"Okay," I said, not wanting to push it. Still, I worried. I knew that Erebus said it would take weeks—maybe even months—for the poison to work its way through Chris's body, but magical fox venom isn't really an exact science.

We needed to get out of Kerberos as quickly as possible so I could heal him. Which meant we had to keep heading toward the mountain.

But the farther we walked, the hotter it became. What little bits of vegetation there were disappeared, until only the occasional cactus remained. The sun shone down on us as if we were inside an oven and it was trying to cook us alive.

I'd always been that one person who never got sunburned, but now my skin felt hot and tight. When I looked at my arm, it was a bright, fiery red. Chris and Danielle were also burned on every place where their skin was exposed. Erebus, of course, was unaffected.

As we continued on, the desert played tricks on us. Every so often, a beautiful fountain of water would pop up out of nowhere. But we ignored them, since the source of all the drinkable water in Kerberos was the

River of Dreams. If I didn't have my water bottle, I would have succumbed to drinking the water from the fountains and found myself passed out in a nightmarish sleep for hours, the unforgiving sun beating down relentlessly on my unconscious body.

All I could do was remind myself to put one foot in front of the other and trek on. But the heat wasn't the only thing that made that difficult—because gnats buzzed everywhere, seeking moisture in my eyes and my mouth. No matter how much I swatted at them, they refused to stay away. I splashed water from my bottle onto my clothes, and that provided enough distraction for the gnats that not as many of them swarmed my eyes and mouth, but no amount of water I drank could chase away the heat. It felt like I would get so burned that my skin would peel straight off my body. And *that* would probably be more pleasant than the pain I was in now.

Eventually, I stopped and stared up at the hot, amber sun. "When's this going to end?" I said, looking at Erebus for an answer. I sounded whiney, but I didn't care. I just wanted to get out of this heat. "The sun has to go down eventually, right?"

"The sun never sets in the desert here," he said, which explained why it hadn't moved from the highest point in the sky since we'd set foot in this area hours ago. "If you stop to rest it just means you'll be in the sun for longer, which will make it worse long-term. So we need to keep going."

"But for *how long*?" I repeated.

"Not much longer."

"That's not a real answer," Danielle chimed in, emptying the remaining water from her bottle onto her face.

Seconds later, the bottle was magically full again. She dumped that on her head, too. Her hair was wet, as if she'd just gotten out of the shower. But given the lack of humidity, it would be dry again in less than five minutes.

"An hour or two, tops," Erebus said. "You'll all survive. So stop complaining, and let's go."

CHAPTER THIRTY-SIX

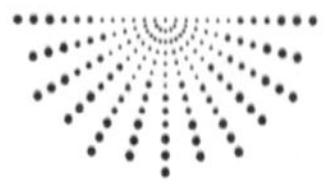

After what felt like *much* longer than two hours, we reached the end of the desert. It ended abruptly, just like all other places we'd traveled through since arriving in Kerberos. One moment we were following the barren path, then we turned around a massive boulder and saw a thriving jungle up ahead.

I ran for the trees, unable to get under their canopied cover fast enough. The moment I reached the shade, I sat on the ground and leaned against one of the trunks, guzzling down as much water as I could manage. The water never truly quenched my thirst in the desert, but now, I finally felt Hydrated again. The air around me was humid and misty, although the mist wasn't nearly as thick as in the Whispering Forest, so we were still able to see. It cooled my skin, making the burn hurt less than it had when exposed straight to the sun.

"Is there anything we can use in here for our sunburn?" Danielle asked, poking through a colorful variety of plants. "Aloe, perhaps?"

"Don't put anything from these plants on your skin," Erebus warned us, and Danielle pulled her hand back, stepping away from the greenery. "There's no predicting *what* they could do. But given where we are, I doubt it would be anything good."

"Where exactly *are* we?" I asked, looking up at the trees. They were gigantic compared to any trees I'd ever seen, their branches and leaves at least three times the size of any on Earth.

Erebus looked at me as if I'd lost my mind. "We're in Kerberos," he said.

"I know that." I glared at him. "But what *area* of Kerberos is this? What type of torture should we expect while we're here?"

"This is the Jungle," Erebus told us. "Like everywhere else in Kerberos, don't consume any food or drink while here. Many variations of food grow here, and while they *will* nourish, each one will come with a different cost. But the food and drink isn't what keeps most people out of the Jungle." He paused to scan the area, as if expecting something to jump out at us at any second.

I stood up and grabbed my bow, wanting to be ready in case anything attacked. I looked at Erebus to continue, but he said nothing.

"Since you clearly want one of us to ask, I'll do the honor," Danielle said, rubbing her hands against her jeans to get rid of any residue from the plants she'd touched. "What keeps most people out of the Jungle?"

"The dragons," Erebus said simply, tossing us each a protein bar and turning to continue along the path.

"*Dragons?*" I repeated, opening my protein bar and hurrying after him. Danielle and Chris did the same. "The same kind of dragons who flew Ethan and Blake up the mountain?"

"Helios's Solar Dragons." Erebus nodded. "They're the only dragons who live in Kerberos. They're the final part of your journey up the mountain. You see—we've taken the path nearly to the end. As you saw when you arrived in Kerberos, the mountain shoots straight up through the clouds. Those clouds are the mist you currently see around you. Soon the path will stop, and the rest of the mountain is a wall straight up to the plateau on top. The wall is impossible to climb. The only way up is a ride from the dragons."

"And you really think those dragons will fly us up the mountain?" Chris asked. "Because in case you forgot, Helios *hates* us. He blames us for killing that cow, and he convinced Ethan to turn against us. Why would his dragons agree to help us?"

"Dragons are notoriously selfish," Erebus said, as if we should have known that already. "If you offer them something that they want badly enough, they'll likely provide their services in return. Remember to be civil and diplomatic while speaking with them, and you'll be fine."

"Hold up." Chris laughed. "These dragons *talk*?"

"Of course dragons talk." Erebus scoffed. "They're some of the most civilized and wisest creatures in the world. Besides gods, obviously."

"That changes everything," Chris said. "Since they talk, I can use the lyre on them."

"That makes sense." Danielle nodded, and turned to Erebus. "What do you think?"

He glanced up and chewed on his lower lip, as if something about the suggestion didn't sit right with him. "I think that's a solid move," he finally said, meeting our gazes again.

"So why did you hesitate?" Danielle asked.

"No reason," he said. "Chris is right. You should use the lyre."

"Okay." I ignored the tension in the air, trying to sound more confident than I felt. "So... where can we find the dragons?"

"At the end of the path," he replied, pointing

forward. "There's a cliff at the point where the Jungle meets the clouds, with a view across the entire realm. It's the dragons' favorite spot in all of Kerberos."

"Then what are we waiting for?" Chris placed his hand on his lyre and puffed out his chest, turning to continue along the path. "Let's go meet these dragons."

CHAPTER THIRTY-SEVEN

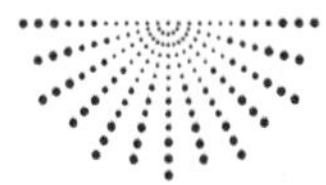

We continued along the path, through the hot and sticky jungle. I sweated out the water in my body as quickly as I could drink it. Sweat soaked my hair and clothes, and it was hard to believe that recently I'd been in a desert, wishing for humidity. Now I felt like I was drowning in the hot, wet air. It was so thick that it was hard to breathe.

Eventually the trees thinned out, opening up into a clearing. When we stepped into it, I saw them—four orange dragons. They were large, but not so large that they dwarfed us. If I reached up, I would be able to touch their heads. They stood next to a cliff, which like Erebus said, looked out over all of Kerberos. When the clouds parted I saw the desert, the Red River, the River of Dreams, and I could just barely make out the Whispering Forest along the horizon.

It was crazy to think about how far we'd traveled to get here.

The dragons watched us with thoughtful, yellow eyes. The largest one stepped forward, observing each of us individually, as if it was trying to size us up.

I swallowed, nervous for whatever was going to happen next. As intimidating as these creatures were, they were majestic as well, and I had no idea what to expect from them.

We continued to stare at each other, and then the dragon in front shifted into human form. The others followed his lead. There were two males and two females. They all had matching yellow eyes, bright fiery hair, and bodies that would make the most beautiful of humans jealous. They were also all naked. I supposed that as dragons, they felt no need for modesty, but I averted my eyes just the same.

"What brings you here?" the dragon who'd shifted first finally spoke, his voice wise and deep.

Chris reached for his lyre and began to play, the notes filling the clearing. But unlike the previous times when he'd played the lyre—when I'd wanted to close my eyes and lose myself in the music—something sounded off. Out of tune. I doubted that people who weren't attuned to music would be able to tell, but I could clearly hear the difference.

"We need a ride to the top of the mountain," Chris said, continuing to pluck and strum the lyre. "The four of you will fly us up there, wait while we complete our task, fly us back down to the portal to Earth, and once we've returned home to Earth you'll forget that you ever met us." He stopped playing the lyre and watched the dragons, waiting for them to follow his command.

I held my breath and gripped my bow, praying that the lyre was still in tune enough to work. Because without the lyre… how were we supposed to convince the dragons to fly us to the top of the mountain?

The male dragon who'd spoken first snorted, a puff of smoke billowing out of his nose. "Why should we do as you say, mortal?" he asked, his voice booming so loudly now that I could feel its vibration in my bones.

"Because the lyre…" Chris glanced back at me, his eyes wide in panic.

One of the female dragons stepped up to join the first. "You thought you could use Apollo's Golden Lyre on *us*?" She sneered. "We are *dragons*. We are not silly creatures who can be wooed by the sound of music. You dare to think us so naïve, so easily pliable? You think you can insult us in this way?"

Chris lowered his hands to the strings, as if to try playing again.

"Don't." I reached for his hand to stop him, speaking as quietly as possible. "The lyre's out of tune. It won't work."

"Then what are we supposed to do?" His eyes were wide, panicked. "We need to get up that mountain."

"Don't you think I know that?" I hissed.

"There's no need to speak so quietly," the first dragon—who I assumed was the leader—said. "Our ears are far more advanced than yours, and we can hear every word."

Danielle stepped up beside me and leveled her gaze with the dragon's. "It was wrong of us to use the lyre, and I apologize on behalf of my group," she said. "We're just in a hurry, and we thought it would be the fastest way to complete our mission. But now that you know why we traveled so far to seek you out, I must ask—is there anything you can do to help us?"

None of the dragons betrayed an ounce of emotion. I leaned back and looked at each of them nervously, but they just watched us as if we were bugs they could easily squash.

"Of course we *can* help you," the leader finally said. "We *can* fly you to the top of the mountain, wait for you to finish whatever you set out to do there, fly you back down to the portal, and allow you to return to Earth. But what we *can* do and what we *want* to do are different things entirely. Just because we *can* do something doesn't mean that we *want* to do it, or that we *will* do it. You see... for us to *want* to do this for you, we need something worthy from you in return."

"And after you tried to manipulate us with the Golden Lyre, what we *want* to do right now is kill you," one of the female dragons added, grinning maliciously.

I looked to Erebus for help, but he stood silently to the side, watching us as if he couldn't care less how this confrontation ended. It didn't make sense. I knew from all the ways he'd helped us so far that he *did* care—why was he acting so nonchalant now?

Primordial deities could be so frustrating sometimes.

But I didn't have time to worry about him right now, so I turned my focus back to the dragons. "What exactly do you want?" I asked the leader. I held tightly onto my bow—I didn't want to use my final crystal arrow, but I wouldn't hesitate if it were necessary. "Everything we have is back on Earth... but perhaps we could make a deal. Tell us what you want, and if we have it, we'll send it back to Kerberos once we've returned home."

"That isn't how these deals work," he said. "*This* is how they work—you must first present a gift to us. Then we will decide if we wish to accept your gift or not. If we accept, we will do as you asked in return. If we do not accept… normally we would let you go on your way. But after you insulted us by attempting to use that instrument to manipulate our thoughts and actions, that will not be the case this time."

"You cannot get away with trickery like that and live," the female added, as if we were too stupid to understand her the first time she'd said so. "Unless, of course, you offer us something tempting enough to change our minds."

"I could give you the lyre," Chris offered, holding it out to them. "The deal would make sense, since the lyre is what angered you in the first place, right?"

"What use have we for that lyre?" The leader sneered. "It only works when tuned, and it can only be tuned by Apollo. Apollo has never stepped foot into Kerberos. And if the portal ever opens, I doubt he would agree to tune it for us. Your offer of an out of tune magical lyre that only works when it's *in* tune is insulting. I hereby reject your offer. And I hope—for your sakes—that you do not propose such an offensive offer again."

The other dragons nodded, clearly in agreement with their leader's sentiments.

"What about my remaining crystal arrow, along with the Golden Bow?" I said. "When the crystal arrow is shot with the Golden Bow, it's guaranteed to hit its target, as long as the target is in sight. Nothing like it exists in the entire world."

"That last fact is true." The leader pressed his lips together and stared down at the arrow in my hand. Finally he raised his gaze to mine, his amber eyes flashing with suspicion. "But does the arrow's magic last indefinitely? I see you have other, similar arrows in your quiver, and yet you say that this one in your hand is the only one of its kind. Which leads me to believe that the magic in the arrow is limited, and the ones in your quiver have already reached that limit."

"The arrow can only be used once," I admitted. "But if you choose when to use it wisely, as I'm sure you would, it could be an extremely useful weapon to have at your disposal."

"The Golden Bow *is* a beautiful weapon," the female purred. "But an arrow with magic that will disappear after one shot is hardly a fair bargain in exchange for a favor from all four of us."

"Per usual, I agree with my mate," the leader said. "Both of your offers thus far have been sub-par. What else do you have to give?"

"Like I said, we have a lot back on Earth," I said, trying to think of *something* we could part with that they might value. "Do you have guns in Kerberos? I haven't seen any so far. They're the most powerful handheld weapons on Earth—with enough bullets, you'll be victorious against any opponent."

"They were locked in Kerberos over three *thousand* years ago," Danielle whispered to me, rolling her eyes. "Guns didn't exist back then. They probably have no idea what they are—"

"Silence!" the leader commanded, and Danielle clasped her mouth shut, stopping mid-sentence. "We've heard of these 'guns' that you speak of, and we have no use for such crude, mortal weapons. What else do you have to offer? Think long and hard, as I'm growing tired of your insolent suggestions."

Danielle reached for the handle of her sword, and I shook my head, trying to will her to stop. We'd trekked through Antarctica for that sword, talked our way into Chione's ice palace, and risked our lives to free it from the block of ice that had encased it for multiple millennia as it waited for the one deemed worthy by the goddess Aphrodite to free it. Danielle—a descendant of Aphrodite herself—had removed it from the ice. That sword was her destiny.

"No." I stepped forward, stopping her before she could pull out the sword. "We have so much back on Earth. We just need to think. What do we have that they might want? There has to be *something*..."

"Our patience is wearing thin," the leader said. "And

we will do nothing for you unless what you offer is in your possession and handed over to us now. So tell us, child," he said, his eyes twinkling with greed as he stared down at Danielle. "What is it that you wish to offer?"

CHAPTER THIRTY-EIGHT

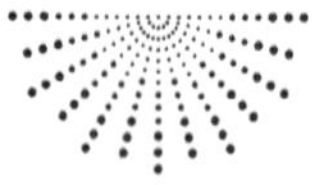

Danielle removed the sword and held it up high, the gold shining so brightly under the amber sun that I had to shield my eyes to protect them from the light. "The Golden Sword of Athena," she said, looking like a goddess herself as she presented the ancient weapon to the dragons. "It was forged by Athena at the beginning of time, and is blessed with the ability to cut through any material in the universe. The Golden Sword is so powerful that the gods locked it away for thousands of years, making it accessible only to the one they deemed worthy to retrieve it. My ancestor Aphrodite cast the spell to lock away the sword, and she chose me as the one to free it, so that I could use it to behead the gorgon Medusa. But I've already completed that task, so if you deem the sword an acceptable trade, I will hand it over to you in return for your services."

The dragons said nothing, practically salivating as they admired the sword.

"The Golden Sword of Athena," the leader finally said, smiling greedily at the item he spoke of. "Every creature on Earth *and* Kerberos has heard of this weapon, but few have seen it with their own eyes." He reached forward and opened his hand, waiting for Danielle to hand over the sword.

She stepped back, moving it out of his reach. "I won't give it to you until you agree to do as we asked," she said.

"Silly girl." He snarled. "You expect us to accept your offer without us first confirming that this is the mythical sword you speak of? Let me hold it first. Then I will decide whether or not to accept your offer."

"You would be able to tell that this is the Golden Sword just by holding it?" I asked him.

"Of course," he said. "You forget, young mortal, what creatures you are speaking to. We are dragons. We know and recognize precious metals better than any creature in the Universe—perhaps even better than the blacksmith god Hephaestus himself."

"It's a good thing that Hephaestus can't hear through

the realms." Erebus chuckled. "Because he would *not* be happy to hear you say that."

"It is the truth." The leader held his head proudly, focusing on Danielle. "Now, will you allow me to inspect the sword, or not?"

"You promise that if you choose not to accept the deal, you'll give the sword back to me?" she asked.

"If this sword is what you say it is, then we *will* be accepting your deal," he said. "You have my word."

"Do you swear it on the gods themselves?" I asked.

"Yes—I swear my word to Zeus and the Olympians."

"Not only the Olympians," I said. "The Olympians don't reside in Kerberos, so swearing to them while here means nothing." I glanced back at Erebus, hoping the human form he'd taken around us wasn't recognizable to any of the creatures here. He nodded—very subtly—so I turned back to the dragon and continued, "Swear on the primordial deities Nyx and Erebus themselves."

The dragon raised an eyebrow. "What do you know of the primordial deities?" he asked.

"I know enough." I held his fiery gaze, refusing to back down. "Why are you stalling? If you intend to keep your word, I don't see why this is a problem."

"Fine." He huffed. "*If* this is the Golden Sword of Athena, then I promise on the primordial deities Nyx and Erebus that I and my companions will accept your deal."

Danielle stepped forward, still holding tightly onto the sword. "Repeat the terms of the deal," she commanded. "To ensure your oath is legitimate." She raised the sword, ready to swing it at the nearest dragon. "If you don't, then I'll demonstrate that this is the Golden Sword of Athena by slicing your friend here in half. Since you've already threatened to kill us, I have nothing to lose if I take him and anyone else I can slice apart down with us, do I?"

"Stand down." The leader narrowed his eyes at Danielle, but she remained where she stood. "If this is the Golden Sword of Athena, then I promise on the primordial deities Nyx and Erebus that I and my three companions with me here now will fly you to the top of the mountain, wait for you while you complete your task up there, and then fly you back down to the portal."

"And not attack us once we're back at the portal," Chris added. "You'll allow us safely through and will mention to no one that you ever saw us. And you also need to specify that you'll take us to each location exactly when we're ready to go there, and no later."

I looked at him, my eyes wide. Not because I was shocked that he was requiring so much from the dragons, but because I was impressed that he was being so detailed in the wording of the agreement. Since the day I met him, I knew that Chris was a good-hearted person, but I hadn't thought of him as particularly *smart*. Perhaps I'd been too quick to judge.

"What?" Chris smiled at me sheepishly, and he shrugged. "It's what Kate would ask of them if she were here with us now."

"True." My eyes watered at the mention of Kate, but I blinked back my tears and turned back to the dragons, not wanting to show them any weakness. "Do you accept our deal?"

The leader pursed his lips, and my heart pounded with fear that he would say no.

"We accept," he finally said, and he repeated the oath with the inclusion of Chris's additions. "You're quite a demanding group of mortals, aren't you?"

"We're offering you the Golden Sword of Athena," I reminded him. "All we're requesting is a fair trade."

"And if this sword isn't actually the Golden Sword, then I don't think we have to spell it out for you again what we'll do to you for your earlier deception, do we?" He raised an eyebrow, and I wondered how stupid he thought we were. Apparently very.

I was beginning to hate dragons more than I had when I'd seen them flying Ethan and Blake to the top of the mountain.

"Let me guess," Chris said, sounding surprisingly cheery. "You'll kill us?"

"Yes," the female hissed. "At least one of you catches on quickly."

"You won't be killing any of us." Danielle lowered the sword and held it out to the leader. "Because this *is* the Golden Sword of Athena. See for yourself."

CHAPTER THIRTY-NINE

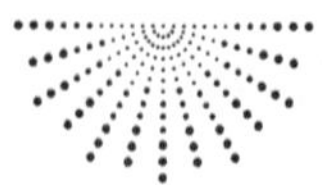

The dragon took the sword and weighed it in his hand, studying it carefully. He held it at multiple angles, examining every inch from the tip to the handle. His expression was blank and impossible to read.

I could barely breathe as I watched him, terrified that he would declare the sword fake and attack us simply for the sake of it.

Eventually, he held up his other hand, extended his claws, and sliced the sword through the longest one. The nail dropped to the ground. The three other dragons all sucked in deep breaths, staring at the fallen nail. None of them moved. Then the leader knelt down, scooped up a handful of dirt, and placed the nail inside. He poured the dirt over the nail, burying it.

Once it was fully covered, he stood back up and

looked at us. "Only the Golden Sword of Athena can slice through a dragon's claw," he said. "You are correct. This *is* the Golden Sword."

"And now it's *ours.*" The female reached for it greedily, but he held it closer, not handing it to her. She frowned and took a step away from him, saying nothing.

"Yes, it's yours." Danielle backed up to join Chris and me, looking wistfully at the sword. "And since you agreed to our terms, you'll shift back into your dragon forms and fly us up the mountain now."

"Mortals." The other male in the group sneered—the one who hadn't spoken up until now. "Are you truly so naïve? The Olympians can't set foot in this realm, the Titans are trapped at the top of the mountain, and the primordial deities stopped caring about what happened to those of us here long ago. In Kerberos, we have no gods. Oaths mean nothing here."

He shifted into dragon form, took a deep breath, and released a blaze of fire from his nostrils. If Blake were here—and if we could access our powers here—he would hold out his hands and shield us from the fire. But Blake wasn't here, and our powers were inaccessible while we weren't on Earth.

So I screamed and turned away, holding my arms up in front of my head as I prepared for the flames to consume me.

CHAPTER FORTY

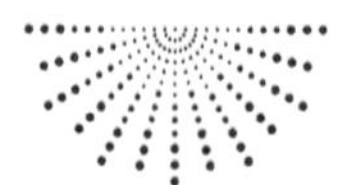

The fire didn't come. The heat was so close that I could feel it on my skin—and then, it was gone.

Was I dead? I'd expected to feel pain—to feel the agonizing torture of those final moments when I burned to death. But there was nothing.

Was dragon fire so powerful that death was instantaneous?

I lowered my arms and opened my eyes, facing the dragons. The three of them in human form were still there, but the one who had shifted back into dragon form and tried to kill us was gone. The only evidence that he'd been there at all was the two large footprints on the ground where he'd stood.

The other female in the group—who I guessed was his mate—screamed and searched the area where he'd been standing, her arms flailing around the empty space. "Where is he?" she yelled, her eyes ablaze. "What did you *do* to him?"

Erebus stepped forward, his gaze dark and unwavering. "Your leader swore an oath to the gods, and the three of you agreed. Your companion broke that oath. Therefore, he has been pulverized."

"The gods deserted us long ago," the female spat. "What do you know of oaths, mortal?"

"I know more than you realize, *dragon*." He spoke the name of her breed as if it were an insult. "And I know that you cannot deny what you saw with your own eyes. You made an oath to the primordial deities Nyx and Erebus. The moment your mate betrayed that oath, he disappeared into darkness itself. Do you wish to test the gods further? Or will you be true to your word and honor your promise?"

She dropped her hands to her sides, fear flashing in her eyes. "If we do as we promised, will my mate be returned?" she asked.

"I cannot say for sure," Erebus said. "But after what you just witnessed, do you really want to test what will happen if you refuse?"

I half-expected her to shift forms and breathe flames at us, so she could join her mate. Instead, she narrowed her eyes and stepped back behind her leader.

"You speak confidently for a mortal," she said, studying Erebus suspiciously.

"I have seen much for my years." His expression betrayed nothing. "You've sworn an oath to the gods, and while they may have ignored Kerberos in the past, they are paying attention now. Try anything else, and you *will* experience their wrath."

The female opened her mouth as if she was going to say more, but her leader interrupted before she could speak.

"The gods are clearly watching out for you," he said to us, holding his hand out to the female in a signal for her to be quiet. "We will not test them again. When do you wish us to fly you to the top of the mountain?"

"We leave now," I said, and he nodded, shifting back to dragon form. He still held the Golden Sword with his front claw.

The other two dragons shifted forms as well. They stretched their wings and raised their necks to the sky, ready to take flight. Then they lowered themselves to the ground—I assumed they wanted us to hop onto their backs.

"Nicole—you ride on the back of the leader," Erebus instructed. "Chris will ride his mate. Danielle and I will be together on the other female." He didn't wait for us to agree—instead, he strolled over to the female, lifted Danielle onto her back, and jumped up to join her.

I hopped onto the back of the leader, and Chris did the same on his mate. Chris winced slightly when putting pressure on his arm, but I looked away, pretending not to notice. There was nothing I could do for him now. The most I could do was to make sure we finished our mission as quickly as possible so we could get back to Earth where I could heal him.

I situated myself on the dragon's back, holding onto the ridges on his neck. He stood up, and the ground grew farther away from me, making my stomach feel like it was rising into my throat. What if I fell off? I'd ridden horses before, but a *dragon*? I didn't even think that dragons existed before entering Kerberos.

It was finally sinking in that we would be *flying*. High above the ground, with nothing strapping me in to keep me safe. I swallowed, feeling like I was about to be sick. I didn't want to do this. But I didn't have a choice. I *had* to do it if I wanted to reach Blake.

So I bent my legs at the knees, using my thigh muscles to put pressure on the dragon's sides to keep my balance, as I would while riding a horse. His scales were sharp and rough, digging into my bare skin.

"Don't let me fall, okay?" I whispered to him, tightening my grip so much that my knuckles turned white.

He didn't reply, instead spreading his wings and running toward the cliff.

The wind rushed past my face and through my hair,

and I screamed as he jumped off the ledge and soared up into the amber sky.

CHAPTER FORTY-ONE

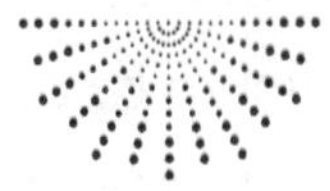

Nothing could have prepared me for what it felt like to ride the back of a flying dragon. Seeing the ground so far away—the trees, the animals, the river—as if they were a toy model instead of the real world, was something I'd experienced before on an airplane. But without the window separating me from the world, without being strapped into a chair or safety net of any kind—it was so terrifying that my head spun and my heart pounded so fast that I felt like it was about to beat right out of my chest. I held onto the dragon with every bit of strength I could muster, keeping my eyes up and praying it would end soon.

We flew higher and higher until we were above the clouds, the amber sun shining down on us so strongly that it scorched my already burned skin. We circled the mountain, which as Erebus told us, was now a straight wall to the top.

Eventually, the cliff reached a plateau, although I couldn't see far due to the trees near the edge. The dragons landed close to the edge, lowering their wings and settling onto the ground so we could hop off their backs. It was a huge relief to be on solid land. My hands tingled from holding onto my dragon so tightly, and I flexed them to get my blood flowing, finally able to feel my fingers again.

My dragon shifted back into human form, and the other two dragons followed his lead. "The Titans are imprisoned in the center of the plateau," he told us. "That is where the others of my kind likely took your friends. We will not go there, as our deal was to bring you to the top of the mountain, which we have done. We will wait for you here and fly you down to the portal once you've returned."

"Thank you," I said, checking my arrows to make sure I hadn't lost any of them during the flight. With only two used arrows and one crystal arrow left, I couldn't afford for anything to happen to them. To my relief, they were all in place.

Danielle eyed up the Golden Sword in the leader's hand. "I don't know what we'll be facing at the center of the mountain, but we'll likely need all of the weapons we can get," she said. "Is there any chance that we can borrow the sword? We'll return it to you the moment we're back."

"We made a deal." The dragon held the sword closer to his side. "This sword is mine now. You will have to manage without it."

"We'll be fine," I told Danielle. "I still have one crystal arrow, and two regular arrows."

"And I have a knife," Chris added. "We all have our knives. Don't forget about those."

"Wonderful." Danielle sighed and looked longingly at the Golden Sword. "How well are the Titans imprisoned again?"

"They're frozen in a lake," Erebus told us. "It's the lake that begins the River of Dreams—the water in it is powerful enough to block their magic."

The female dragon whose mate he'd pulverized raised an eyebrow at him. "The top of the mountain is rarely visited," she said. "How do you know all of this information?"

"I have my ways," he said, and then he turned and led us into the forest, not allowing the dragons to ask any more questions.

CHAPTER FORTY-TWO

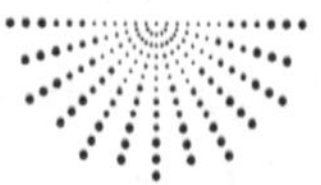

We walked through the forest, the air growing colder and colder until I had to wrap my arms around myself to keep from shivering. The trees went from full and green to brown and bare, as if within an hour we'd traveled from summer to winter. Instead of leaves, icicles hung from the branches. It would have felt like a winter wonderland if it hadn't been for an eerie emptiness that filled the forest, the coldness a sharp warning of danger that penetrated my bones.

Eventually, the forest ended, and we stepped into a clearing with a lake in the center. In the middle of the lake, twelve creatures as large as giants were frozen from the waist down. As still and as pale as corpses, most of them had their eyes closed, but a few stared out into the forest, their gazes empty and hollow. The ice had entrapped them. But lines spider webbed along the outside edge of the lake—cracks. The cracks weren't close to the center yet, but it looked like in time, they would make it there.

I froze where I stood, not wanting to alert the creatures to our presence.

"The twelve first generation Titans," Erebus explained, keeping his voice low. "As I already mentioned, they've been frozen in the lake since they were forced into Kerberos. Their powers are blocked, and after so many years of torture, they've lost themselves to their own minds. They won't know you're here unless you step foot onto the lake."

"It's cracking," Danielle mentioned what I'd already observed. "What happens when the cracks reach the Titans? Will they get their powers back? Will they be freed?"

"The cracks started forming on the night of the Olympian Comet," Erebus told us. "There's no saying when they'll reach the center, but my guess is the summer solstice. Once that happens, the Titans will be able to escape their imprisonment, and the portal will be fully open, so they'll be able to go back through to Earth."

"That's not going to happen," Chris said, gripping

the handle of his knife. "Well—maybe they'll escape the lake, but we'll close the portal first."

"Yes," Danielle agreed. "Although it would be nice if we actually knew *how* we're supposed to close the portal." She glanced sideways at Erebus, not so subtly hinting that she wanted him to tell us.

"I'm not telling you now," he said. "You're not ready yet. It would only distract you from the task you came here to complete."

"Erebus is right," I said. "We have to focus on doing what we came here to do—getting back Blake and Medusa's head. Once we're back on Earth, then we'll turn Typhon to stone and figure out how to seal the portal. Since we can't seal the portal until we're back, it doesn't do us any good to worry about it now."

Danielle nodded, although she didn't look convinced.

Then I heard something from off in the distance—clapping. I turned to look where it was coming from, and saw Ethan standing on the top of a hill, in front of a small cabin. He smirked as he stared down at us, and continued to clap, finally stopping once he had our full attention.

"I didn't think you would have the guts to follow me into Kerberos," he said, his voice booming across the clearing. "Looks like you proved me wrong."

Two people I didn't recognize emerged from the

cabin to stand on both sides of him—a man and a woman. From their bright red hair and lack of clothing, I assumed they were dragons. Likely the same two dragons that flew him and Blake to the top of the mountain.

I steadied my bow at the sight of them, the crystal arrow strung through and ready to shoot. These weren't the same dragons who had made a deal with us—they owed us nothing. There was no reason to think they wouldn't attack on the spot. And without them having sworn an oath to Erebus, the god wouldn't be able to stop them like he'd done to the dragon who had gone back on his word in the Jungle.

"Helios instructed these two dragons of his to protect me," Ethan explained, motioning to the dragons by his sides. "We knew you'd followed us through the portal the moment one of Apollo's crystal arrows shot past us on our flight up here. I figured you would try to reach the top of the mountain, so I've been waiting for you, just in case you made it this far. I doubted you would." He paused to study us, a manic smile crossing his face. "But I'm happy you did," he continued. "Because there's something inside that I've been *dying* to show you."

CHAPTER FORTY-THREE

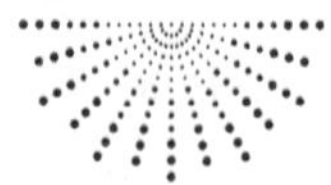

Moving faster than a human could comprehend, I replaced the crystal arrow with a used arrow and shot it through the heart of the male dragon. Then I grabbed the second used arrow, strung it through my bow, and shot it through the heart of the female.

They both fell to the ground—dead.

Ethan glared at me, his hands tightening by his sides. "What was that for?" he asked, glancing at the slayed dragons. "After the sacrifice I made when I got here, Helios would have forgiven you all for killing his immortal cow on his island. Now that you killed two of his dragons... I can't imagine that truce will still stand."

"What are you talking about?" I pointed my remaining arrow—the crystal one—at Ethan's heart. "And where's Blake?"

Blake would have come running to us the moment he heard our voices, so I could only guess that he was being kept somewhere else. And since Ethan was the only one who might know where that place was, I had to keep him alive.

For now.

But despite everything I'd said back in the cave about wanting Ethan dead, now that I knew about the endless dark torture that would await him in the underworld of Kerberos, I wasn't sure that I could do it. Because Ethan was still one of us—a demigod. Before his sister had died, he'd helped us fight in Greece. He'd risked his life for us. I couldn't just forget about that as if it had never happened at all.

He'd made bad choices, but he wasn't a monster. If someone I loved had been taken from me like his sister had been taken from him, and if a god told me they could bring them back… I don't imagine an offer like that would be easy to turn down. I wanted to think that I would have the strength to put the fate of the world before a single life, even the life of someone I loved. But I couldn't know *what* I would do in a situation like Ethan's, because I'd never had to face it.

Yes, he'd made a huge mistake. But it wasn't over yet. He could still tell us where Blake was, and return Medusa's head.

He deserved a chance to redeem himself.

"Answer my question," I told him, zeroing in on his heart. Even though I didn't plan on killing him, I couldn't let him see my bluff. "Where's Blake?"

"And Medusa's head," Chris added.

"That's what I wanted to show you," Ethan said, still smiling maniacally. "And it's why I'm so happy you're here."

"The dragons who were here to protect you are dead," I reminded him, pulling back on the string of my bow. "We have the upper hand now. So stop stalling, and answer our questions."

"I suppose you do deserve an answer." He stepped aside, motioning to the door of the cabin. "So here it is. Blake and Medusa's head… they're both inside. Go in and see for yourselves."

CHAPTER FORTY-FOUR

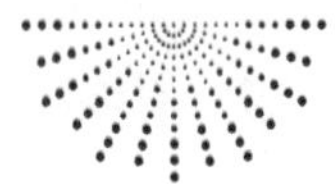

Fighting my instinct to run straight into the cabin to see Blake, I adjusted my target and sent the arrow soaring toward it. Ethan must have had quick reflexes—I supposed it made sense, because he was a demigod as well—and he whizzed out of the way when the arrow came toward him.

But the arrow turned to adjust its path, as if it had a mind of its own, and buried itself straight into my intended destination.

Ethan screamed and fell to the ground, his hands flying to his knee. He yanked the arrow out and tried to stand up, but he didn't get far before crashing back down. He grunted and tried again, managing to slowly stand and balance on his good leg. He took one hop toward us and groaned again from the pain, although he sucked it up and took another hop. He stared at me, his eyes murderous and livid. I had no doubt that he wanted me dead.

I hurried to one of the fallen dragons, yanked the arrow out of her heart, and strung it through my bow. From this angle, shooting it through Ethan's other knee was easy.

He screamed again and fell back onto the ground.

With both kneecaps busted, he wouldn't be able to walk. But I didn't have any more time to pay attention to Ethan, because Blake was inside that cabin.

I ran for the door, moving with demigod speed, anxious to see him again. This was it. The moment when Blake and I would be reunited.

But Erebus appeared in front of me before I could blink, blocking my path.

"What are you doing?" I tried to run around him, but he was faster than me, and he held his arms out to stop me. "Let me through!"

"I can't do that." He placed his hands on my shoulders to hold me still, his eyes serious. "Ethan said that Medusa's head is in there, too. For all you know, he positioned the head so it's staring at the door—so anyone who enters will be turned to stone. I'm the only one here who's immune to Medusa's gaze. You have to let me go in first."

"A trap like that would be a good idea." Ethan laughed from his place on the ground, holding his hands over his kneecaps to stop the blood from pouring out. "But it's not what I did. What I did is even better. And I can't *wait* to see your reaction when you see it for yourself."

I opened my mouth to ask what he *did* do, but I stopped myself. Nothing that Ethan said could be trusted. And as much as I hated to admit it, Erebus was right. He had to go first to make sure that it was safe.

"Blake!" I yelled through the door and pounded my fists against it, hoping he could hear me. "We're sending in Erebus first. He's on our side. Once he checks out the inside of the cabin, I'm coming in right after him."

There was no response. My heart dropped, and I stared helplessly at the door. I hoped that if anything, I would at least hear his voice. Blake would have answered me if he were in there.

Which meant one thing—Ethan was lying. Blake *wasn't* in the cabin.

In that case, I was glad that I'd shot Ethan in the kneecap and not in the heart. I needed him alive so he could tell us where Blake *really* was.

Erebus dissolved into shadow form, leaving me outside in front of the cabin. Danielle and Chris stood behind me. I glanced over at Ethan, hoping to see a trace of humanity on his face, but he just watched me, still smiling like a crazy person, his eyes glowing with hatred.

What happened to the Ethan that I'd met on the Land of the Lotus Eaters, who had fought with us against Scylla and Charybdis, and had been by our side as we acquired the immortal milk from Helios's island? We didn't know him for long, but he had been our friend. I knew I hadn't imagined that.

But after his sister died, he'd twisted into someone I didn't recognize. There was no point in trying to convince him that Rachael's death wasn't my fault—that he didn't have to punish us to get her back. He was too far gone for us to reason with him. He would never stop blaming me for what happened to her. We would never be safe as long as he was alive.

Every instinct in my body told me to finish the job and kill him. But I couldn't—not without being sure about what happened to Blake. I also still hated the idea of sending him to the underworld here, no matter how awful he'd been to us. So I turned away from him and marched to the other fallen dragon, pulling the arrow out of his heart and placing it into my quiver. Then I walked back over to stand with Chris and Danielle.

"Once we get Blake and Medusa's head, we'll finish off Ethan and fly back with our dragons," Chris said, his voice strong and sure. "We'll never have to worry about him coming after us again."

"No one deserves to go to the underworld here," Danielle cut in. "Maybe we should just leave him here on the mountain. He won't be able to get down with his knees busted up like that. We'll close the portal, and he'll be stuck here with all the other monsters who turned against the Olympians in the Second Rebellion, never able to return to Earth again."

"I agree with Danielle," I said. "I would send him to Hades in a heartbeat... but the underworld here? I don't know if I could live with myself if we did that."

"If we left him here, what would stop Helios's dragons from getting him and flying him back to the portal before we have time to close it?" Chris asked. "We can't leave him alive. Not after everything he's done. It's too risky."

"You're both right." I sighed, pacing around in front of the cabin. What was taking Erebus so long? "But as of right now, we still need Ethan alive. We can't kill him until we find Blake."

"You don't want to kill me," Ethan grumbled. "Once Helios finds out, he'll come for revenge the moment you step foot back on Earth."

"Do you really think Helios cares about you?" I reached for one of the arrows protruding from his knee and yanked it out, enjoying the pain in his scream. I yanked out the other arrow as well. I didn't even bother to wipe off his blood before sticking the arrows back into my quiver. "Helios just needed you to do his dirty work for him," I continued. "You were a pawn to him—that's all. Someone he could manipulate. Now that you've done what he wanted, I doubt he's even trying to get your sister back for you."

"You're wrong." Ethan held himself up on his elbows, gritting his teeth as he spoke. Sweat dripped down his face from the pain of his injuries. "Helios *will* get my sister back. And once he does, she'll *kill* you for what you did to her."

I turned my back to him, since what was the point of responding? Rachael wasn't coming back. And even if she did, I hoped that unlike her brother, she would see reason and realize that her death wasn't my fault.

After all, the fight with the Hydra would have gone differently if she hadn't deviated from the plan and impulsively run to fight it without any backup.

Before I could think about it any more, Erebus appeared outside the cabin, his expression grim. My breath caught at the sight of him. I wanted to ask what was in there… but dread filled my chest at the possibility of what I might find out.

Instead, I just watched him, waiting for his report.

"Medusa's head has been destroyed," he said, not meeting my eyes. "It won't turn anyone to stone ever again."

"And Blake?" I swallowed, terrified about whatever I

was about to hear. But I couldn't wait any longer. I needed to know the truth.

"He's dead." Ethan laughed, his twisted, dark expression making my heart sink into my stomach. "I killed him."

CHAPTER FORTY-FIVE

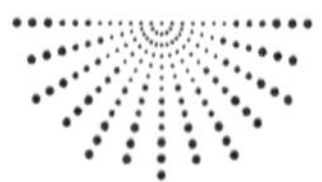

"You couldn't have," I said, refusing to believe it. "Blake's strong. He would have fought you."

"He *is* strong." Ethan nodded, still smiling. "But you forget—I'm a demigod. I'm stronger. *And* I had the dragons on my side."

I opened the door to the cabin, preparing to prove him wrong.

The world collapsed around me at what I saw inside.

Blake lay in the center of the cabin, his eyes closed, surrounded by a pool of his blood. Cuts covered every bit of his skin—some of them shallow, some of them deep. Blood was all over his body. It soaked his clothes. So much blood, everywhere.

"Blake." I said his name softly and hurried over to

him, resting my hand on his arm. He had to wake up. He *had* to. He couldn't be dead. Not here… not in Kerberos. He'd been hurt, yes, and he'd lost a lot of blood, but he was strong. He *would* get better.

Except that his body was cold. Normally, he exuded so much warmth, but there was none of that now. There were so many cuts, and so much blood.

"No." My throat closed up, and I could barely get the word out. Tears streamed down my face and onto his chest. I couldn't breathe… I couldn't think. "You can't be gone," I said, shaking his arm to try to get him to wake up. "This can't be real. I can't keep fighting without you. I love you, Blake. I never got to tell you, but I love you so much." I bit down on my lip and placed both hands on his chest, searching for a heart-beat. Searching for *anything* to prove that he was still alive.

There was nothing.

His chest was cold, his heart still.

But I couldn't give up. Because despite not being able to use our powers in Kerberos, and despite never being able to bring someone back from death before, I had to try to heal him.

No… I had to do more than try. I had to succeed. Because I couldn't lose Blake. Not like this.

If I couldn't heal Blake when he needed me most, what good was I at all?

I closed my eyes and reached out with my mind, trying to locate white energy in the air around me. I searched and searched, pushing harder than I ever had before. But it was like floating in a vacuum. I couldn't feel anything there.

I couldn't access my powers.

I collapsed onto Blake's chest, the tears coming so quickly that I didn't think they would ever stop. Time stood still. Numbness sank deep into my bones, and I felt as cold as Blake. I couldn't move. I couldn't think. All I could do was bury my face in his chest and cry.

How was I supposed to continue on this mission without him? He'd been beside me from the moment I first discovered my powers. He'd helped me understand them, and helped me learn how to be as strong as I could be. He fought beside me, and protected me, and was there for me no matter what.

I loved him. And even though I hadn't told him yet, and he hadn't told me yet, I knew in my heart that he loved me, too.

How could I accept that he was gone? That I would never see him again?

I couldn't.

I *wouldn't.*

Because no soul was ever truly gone. Erebus had told us that himself on our way up the mountain. So I sat back up and wiped the tears off my face. Danielle was beside me—she was crying, too. Chris gripped the handle of his knife, looking ready to destroy whoever had done this to Blake.

I had nothing to say to either of them right now. Instead, I focused on Erebus. He held the mutilated head of Medusa in his hands—her eyes had been gouged out, making her useless. But I didn't care about that right now. There was only one thing I cared about —Blake.

And so I leveled my gaze with Erebus's and asked, "How do we get to the underworld of Kerberos?"

CHAPTER FORTY-SIX

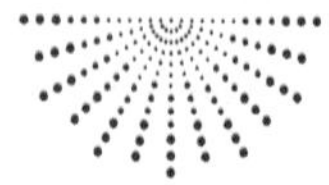

"You don't," Erebus answered, not missing a beat. "Unless you die in Kerberos, there's no other way to get to the underworld. And once there, no one has ever escaped. It's impossible."

Could I die for the chance of finding Blake in the underworld, and do the impossible to figure a way out? I *wanted* to. If there was a chance to be with Blake again, I wanted to have it.

But my family was waiting for me back home. My mom, my dad, and my sister. I loved Blake, but I loved my family, too. I couldn't leave them like that. I would never be able to forgive myself for it.

"There has to be an entrance," I said instead. "A way to get in without dying. There's an entrance to Hades from Earth, right? And Kerberos is a parallel dimension of Earth. So there must be an entrance to the underworld from here."

"That's not how it works," Erebus said. "Kerberos is a *prison world* that can be reached from Earth—not a parallel world. Once someone dies in Kerberos, they're gone forever."

"Not gone," I corrected him. "You said yourself that no one is ever truly gone. They're just trapped in the underworld. Lost, but not gone."

"Being in the underworld of Kerberos is the same as being gone," Erebus said.

"No." I shook my head, refusing to believe it.

"Yes," he said. "And with Medusa's head destroyed, there's no stopping Typhon now. He will rise, you will fail to seal the portal, the Titans will return, and Earth will be destroyed. There's no other possible path. You've failed."

"Then my family's dead anyway." I reached for Blake's cold, dead, bloodied hand, a new wave of tears escaping when I felt how lifeless he was. "Maybe I should just go outside and ask Ethan to kill me. I'm sure he would be happy to do it. Then I could be with Blake."

"Weren't you listening when I told you what the underworld is like here?" Erebus asked. "You wouldn't be *joining* Blake. You would both be two souls floating in the darkness, never able to meet or interact. You would be condemning yourself to an eternity of emptiness."

"So then what else is there left for us to do?" I asked. "Go back to Earth and die there, so we can be with our family in Hades?"

"*If* Hades still exists after the Titans take over," Erebus said. "I wouldn't put it past the Titans to destroy the underworld, too."

"So we failed," Chris said. "All because we decided to trust that backstabbing son of Zeus out there. He's the reason Kate's gone, he's the reason Blake's gone, and he's the reason that the *whole world* will soon be gone." He held up his knife, his eyes gleaming with hatred. "I'm going out there to bury this knife in his heart myself."

"Yes." I nodded, regretting that I'd shot Ethan in the knee and not the heart. "Do it."

He nodded and headed toward the door. I would go out there to help him, or to do it myself, but I couldn't leave Blake here alone. I worried that if I let him out of my sight for even one second, he would be gone. And I refused to leave him here in Kerberos.

Instead, I would bring his body back with us to Earth. I might not be able to bring people back from the dead yet, but I would work on it. After all, I could use my power to kill. With enough practice, why couldn't I use my power to bring people back to life, too?

"Wait," Danielle said, stopping Chris in his tracks. "What if there's still a way we can fix this?"

"There's no way to fix this," Erebus said. "I've already told you—you've failed. From this point forward, there's no possible path that will lead to the future you desire."

"Which is why we won't fix it from this point." Danielle looked off to the side, the gears practically turning in her head as she spoke. "But what if we can go back and fix it from the past?"

"I'm listening." Erebus leaned against the wall and crossed his arms, his gaze locked on Danielle's.

"First of all, answer this," Danielle said to him. "Do you know all of the other primordial deities?"

"Yes—of course," he said. "We're the oldest beings in the Universe. It would be impossible for us *not* to have met at one point or another."

"Can you contact them at all?"

"Sure," he said. "If we feel like reaching out, and if they feel like listening. But there's no promising that both of those things will happen."

Danielle stood up, her hands clenched at her sides, her eyes gleaming with determination. She faced Erebus as an equal—not as a mortal speaking to a god.

And he held his gaze with hers, seeming intrigued by her every word.

"Do you think you can contact Chronos?" she asked him, calmly and steadily.

"Chronos," Erebus repeated, saying the name as if remembering an old friend. "I'll see what I can do."

Then he dissolved into a shadow, and was gone.

CHAPTER FORTY-SEVEN

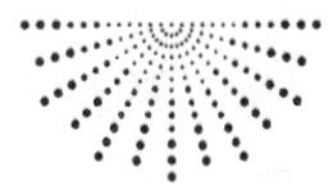

"Who's Chronos?" I looked to Danielle for answers, not letting go of Blake's cold hand.

Before she had a chance to answer, Erebus reappeared in the same place he was standing earlier—except this time he was joined by an older man with gray hair, a long gray beard, wise eyes, and an unearthly glow.

"I am Chronos," the man answered. "The primordial deity of time itself."

I blinked, taking in what he'd said. "You can control time?" I asked him, hope rising in my chest. "You can change the past?"

"I cannot 'control time,'" he said with a kind smile. "Time is an essence that cannot be controlled—not even by the gods. I can, however, travel through the fourth dimension and access any point in the past. Once there, I can make changes as I see fit. Although I try not to change much, since messing with time can get quite complicated, even for a primordial deity like myself."

"But since you came here so quickly, it means you see why we need to make changes, right?" Chris asked.

"We didn't come here 'quickly.'" Erebus chuckled, his eyes dark. "It took me weeks to convince Chronos to meet with me. By then, the spring equinox had passed, and Typhon had risen from Mount Etna. Despite all of the destruction, and despite my telling him that the rise of the Titans was inevitable, Chronos insisted that there was still a chance that the three of you would close the portal. He gave me no choice but to wait it out. Once the three of you failed, he gave in and brought us back here."

"Back up a second." Danielle held up a hand, her forehead wrinkled. "You can *travel through time*. So why did you have to wait for those weeks to pass? Couldn't you have just popped into the future, taken a look at what happened, and then come back?"

"The future is not written in stone," Chronos said, watching her calmly. "There are many possible paths that the future can take at any given time, and those paths are constantly changing based on every decision made. Even deities like Nyx and Erebus, who can see where those paths might lead, are not always correct. The future is in constant flux, and it doesn't exist yet. Therefore, I can only travel to the past. The moment I make myself known in the past and create changes, that moment becomes the present. It's impossible to predict exactly which future those changes will create until the present plays out on its own."

"So when Erebus found you, and both of you saw us fail to close the portal by the summer solstice, *that* was the present," I said, doing my best to understand this. "But since you traveled back to this point in the past, *this* is now the present? And the future that you saw is erased?"

"Precisely." Chronos smiled. "Do you see now why I avoid changing the past?"

"I guess," I said, although it was definitely still confusing. "But you're here now, so that must mean you want to help us. Right?"

"The point when Medusa's head was destroyed seems to be the moment that the rise of the Titans became inevitable," Chronos said. "So yes, I will allow the three of you to travel back in time to a moment when you can retrieve Medusa's head while it was still intact."

"We can save Blake," I whispered.

"And Kate," Chris added. "Don't forget about Kate."

"You're right," I told him, smiling. "We can go back

to before we beheaded Medusa, and we can save both of them. We'll go back to the day before the fight in LA. Then we can do whatever we need to stop Ethan from going through with his crazy plan, and warn Kate about what will happen to her so she can take proper precautions. We'll have both of them back. It'll be like the past nightmarish week never even happened."

"I'm afraid that I can't allow you to go that far back," Chronos told us, his eyes sad.

"Why not?" I dropped Blake's hand and stood up, looking at Chronos straight on. "You're the god of *time*. You just said you could send us back. So why can't we go back to that moment?"

"I said I would send you back to retrieve Medusa's head *before it was destroyed*," he corrected me. "But I absolutely cannot send you back to before you beheaded her. If I do, there's a chance that something else will happen during that fight that will result in an even worse situation—such as Medusa being victorious and turning you all to stone. It's a risk we cannot take."

"We defeated Medusa once," Chris said, slashing his knife through the air. "We can do it again. *Especially* since this time, Ethan won't be there to sabotage us."

"I'm sorry." Chronos shook his head. "Since you were already successful in beheading Medusa in this timeline, I will not send you back to before that moment. We can't risk having any other possible outcome from that fight."

"Then when *will* we go back to?" I asked.

"You will go back to the latest moment possible, as to cause the least number of changes in the timeline," he said. "You will go back to Kerberos, right after Ethan steps through the portal with Blake. Ethan closed Medusa's eyes before coming through the portal and he put her head back in his bag, so you won't be in danger of catching her gaze and turning to stone. You can take care of Ethan, retrieve Medusa's head, and bring it back from Kerberos."

"And Blake will be okay," I said, more than ready to erase these past few days forever.

"Yes." Chronos nodded. "I'm doing this to help you acquire Medusa's head, and one of the side effects will be that Blake will still be alive. But—" he said, looking seriously at the three of us. "When Helios allowed Ethan and his dragons to kill Blake, he considered that to be punishment for all of you after what you did to his cattle. A life for a life. Once you change the past, you will change that, too. Helios will still be looking to punish you. And while the group of you are powerful, you are not powerful enough to take down a god. Only another god is strong enough to do that."

I reached for the sun pendant on my necklace, holding it between my fingers. "Luckily, we have some gods on our side," I said, thinking back to those few minutes when Apollo had visited us in the cave. "Hopefully my father will be willing to help."

"We have my ancestor, and Chris's, too," Danielle added. "Aphrodite and Zeus. And Blake's ancestor…" She glanced at his body and quickly turned away, as if it pained her too much to see him this way. "Who *is* his godly ancestor? No one ever told us."

"Ares," Erebus answered, as if it should have been obvious. "The god of war."

"Sounds like the kind of god we need on our side," Chris said, and I nodded in agreement.

"And what about you?" Danielle asked Erebus, stepping toward him. She reached for his hands, but stopped herself, dropping her arms back to her side. "You've done so much for us already… and you have no idea how grateful I am… but you're not just going to leave. Right?"

"If I don't travel through the time portal with you, then I will forget ever having met you," he said. Danielle's lip quivered, as if she were about to cry, and he added, "That's not what I want to happen, so I will be traveling back with you. Once we're there, I will disappear into the shadows and distract Helios's Solar Dragons to ensure that they don't arrive to pick up Ethan and Blake while you're still there. Once you've taken care of Ethan, retrieved Medusa's head, and have returned to Earth, my role as your guide through Kerberos will be over."

"Will we ever see you again?" Danielle asked.

"I can't say for sure," he said. "And I refuse to make you any promises that I cannot keep. I respect you too much to do that."

They stared at each other for a few seconds, neither of them saying a word. The way they were looking at each other made me think of me and Blake, when we first met but didn't think we could be together.

I didn't doubt that Danielle could have developed feelings for Erebus. After all, he was a *god*. But did he return those feelings? I wouldn't have thought it was possible—not because of anything Danielle had done—but because I couldn't imagine a primordial deity having any interest in a mortal.

But the way he was looking at her right now, as if the thought of never seeing her again would be more torturous than an eternity spent in the underworld of Kerberos, made me wonder.

"I have a question," Chris said, interrupting whatever moment was happening between Erebus and Danielle. "After we travel back in time, what happens to the versions of ourselves that already exist there? We can't co-exist with them, right? So will we have to kill our alternate selves or something crazy like that to make sure the timeline continues like it should?"

"No." Chronos chuckled. "The moment you come face to face with the versions of yourselves from the past, they will cease to exist."

"And Blake?" I asked, although I continued before Chronos could answer, already coming to my own conclusion. "We have to destroy his body. We can't risk the chance of any creature from Kerberos bringing it back in time and showing it to the version of Blake from the past—the version of him that's *alive*. If they do, Blake will be gone. Forever."

"I can turn him to shadow," Erebus offered. "Then no creature alive will be able to get their hands on him."

I glanced at Danielle and Chris, who both nodded. "Yes," I said to Erebus. "That would be helpful. Thank you."

Chronos held his hands up, motioning for us to be quiet. "All of you are not thinking fourth dimensionally," he said, and I focused on him, wondering what on Earth he was talking about. "Once you step through the time portal and land in the past, everything you just experienced from that point until now will be erased. Nothing from then until now will exist anymore—including the boy's body."

"Oh," I said. "Okay. So we won't have to worry about what to do with the Ethan from right now, either?" I glanced at the door, knowing he sat just outside, crippled from my arrows. "He'll just be gone?"

"Precisely." Chronos nodded. "Now you're getting the hang of it."

"So what are we waiting for?" Chris held his gaze with Chronos's, still gripping his knife in his hand. "Let's do this."

"Not so fast," Chronos said. "Before you go, you need to understand that mortals are not meant to travel through time. I am only agreeing to do this for you because we're in dire circumstances, and I cannot think of any other solution that will give us this chance."

"And we thank you for this opportunity," I told him. "We won't let you down. We promise."

"That's not all," he continued, unfazed by my words. "I need to warn you that if you go through with this, there will be a cost."

CHAPTER FORTY-EIGHT

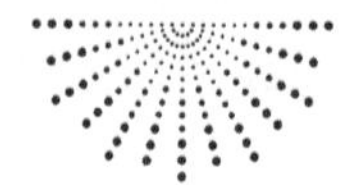

"What kind of cost?" I asked.

He looked seriously at each of us, and said, "The stress of the journey will take away one year of each of your natural lives. Is that something you're willing to risk?"

"Of course I'm willing to risk it." I didn't have to think twice. "One year of my life is worth saving Blake's."

"And it's worth saving the world," Chris added.

We both looked at Danielle, expecting her to agree, too. But she stared down at Blake's body, her eyes far off and her forehead crinkled.

After a few seconds, she looked back up at Chronos. "What will happen if we don't *have* a year of our lives left?" she asked him. "Will we drop dead the moment we step through the time portal?"

"The year is one year from your *natural* lives," he clarified. "You will physically be one year older when you emerge from the portal than you were when you stepped through. You're all young, so if you don't die from unnatural causes, it's reasonable to assume that this won't affect you until far in the future."

"Wait." Chris reached for his shoulder, where a tiny bit of fresh blood was seeping through his shirt. "I was bitten by a fox on the mountain," he told Chronos. "Its poison is in my system. And the poison takes weeks, or maybe months, to kill." He turned to face Danielle and me, his eyes shining with regret. "I don't have a year left," he said. "I can't go back with you. You're going to have to do this on your own."

"No," I said. "We can't just leave you here."

"It won't be like that," he said. "Don't you remember what Chronos told us? About thinking fourth dimensionally? You won't be 'leaving me here,' because I'll never have *been* here in the first place. You'll get to Kerberos right when Ethan comes through the portal with Blake. At that point in time, the past version of me will still be in the cave with the past versions of you and Danielle, speaking to Apollo. After the two of you and Blake take care of Ethan, go back through the portal. When Apollo sees you come through and the past versions of yourselves disappear, you can tell him—and me and Blake—about everything that happened. You can try to get Apollo's help."

"Good idea," Danielle said, walking across the room to pick up Ethan's discarded knife. He must have been so confident that he could beat us with the dragons that he hadn't bothered bringing it outside with him. It wasn't as glamorous as the Golden Sword, but at least it would give her extra protection.

"It is," I agreed. "Especially since it sounds like with everything we'll be up against, we'll *need* Apollo's help against Helios."

"So only three of you will be going through the time portal," Chronos clarified. "Nicole, Danielle, and Erebus."

"Yes." I nodded, and Danielle and Erebus echoed their agreements. "That's right."

"Very well," he said, and then a shimmering pink portal appeared in the center of the cabin. Looking through it, I could see the place where we'd first arrived in Kerberos, just as Ethan stepped through the portal with Blake.

Blake was there—alive. My eyes filled with tears at the sight of him, and I realized that until this moment, I hadn't completely believed that changing the past would be possible.

Seeing him now, I knew that it was.

I glanced over my shoulder for a final look at his

corpse that was here. No matter what, I would *never* allow this future to become reality. It was too painful to live through again. I would have to live with the memory of it forever, and I knew that everything I'd experienced here would haunt me for the rest of my life, but I was more than ready to leave this timeline behind—to erase it from existence.

I'd just looked into the past and seen Blake alive. I was going to make sure he stayed that way.

"Good luck," Chris said, nodding at us and stepping back to stand next to Chronos. "Make sure to tell my past self how brave I was during our adventures here. Don't leave any details out, all right?"

"I promise," I told him. "We'll see you on the other side."

And then I turned back around and stepped through the portal.

FROM THE AUTHOR

I hope you enjoyed *Elementals 4: The Portal to Kerberos!* If so, I'd love if you left a review. Reviews help readers find the book, and I read each and every one of them.

But the Elementals series isn't over yet! There are five books in the series. The final book is *The Hands of Time,* and you can turn the page to read the first three chapters now.

Enjoy!

ELEMENTALS 5: THE HANDS OF TIME

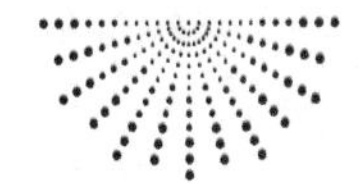

CHAPTER ONE

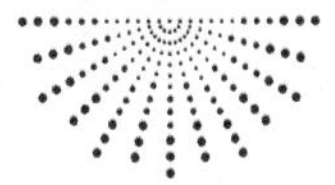

I stepped into the swirling time portal and screamed. My soul felt like it was being torn from my body. It was like someone had reached inside of me, grabbed onto my soul, and was peeling it out of every inch of my skin. I was floating through nothingness, unable to see anything around me, unable to feel anything but the excruciating pain.

I'd traveled through many portals before—ones that had taken me to the cave in Kinsley, to Greece, to Antarctica, to LA, and even to the prison dimension of Kerberos.

None of them had felt like they were tearing me to shreds. Was this portal killing me? Chronos had told us that traveling through the time portal would take away one year of our natural lives. Did I not have one year left? Was this pain happening because I was dying? Was this what death felt like?

Then, as quickly as the pain began, it stopped. Solid ground formed under my feet, and I found myself back in Kerberos, standing next to Danielle, staring at the backs of Ethan and Blake's heads as they waited next to the portal that had taken them to the prison world. Ethan's grip was tight around Blake's body, his knife pressed to his neck.

But despite the danger, all I cared about was that Blake was here. *Alive*. Happiness flooded through me at the sight of him, making all the pain from the time portal disappear at once.

A shadow glided ahead and floated off to the side—Erebus. As promised, he'd shifted into shadow form immediately after coming through the time portal, and was off to distract the dragons.

Then Ethan's knife vanished from his hand.

"Hey!" He flexed his hand and stared at it, as if that might make it appear again. "What happened to my knife?"

Taking advantage of the moment of surprise, Blake elbowed Ethan in the stomach, head-butted him in the chin, and escaped his grasp. He spun around, slamming his fist into Ethan's face over and over again. They were so involved in fighting that they didn't even see Danielle and me standing to the side.

I raised my bow, an arrow already strung through and ready to shoot. But I had no more magic arrows left, and the guys were so close to each other as they fought that I couldn't risk aiming for Ethan and accidentally shooting Blake instead. So I stood ready, waiting for my perfect opportunity to strike.

Ethan spun around and aimed a punch at Blake, but he must have been dizzy from the blows to the head, because he missed. Blake ripped the bag with Medusa's head in it off Ethan's back, tossed it to the side, and got another punch in to his cheek. Danielle hurried to the bag and grabbed it. I followed behind her, my arrow still poised and ready to shoot.

Ethan spat blood to the ground and looked up, finally catching sight of Danielle and me.

"Nicole?" He rubbed his head and glanced at the portal that led back to Earth. "Danielle? But you didn't come through the portal. I would have seen it…I was watching. How did you get here…?"

Blake dropped his fists the moment Ethan said my name, turning to look at me. He looked just as confused to see me as Ethan did. I didn't blame him—after all, Danielle and I had just literally appeared out of thin air.

Danielle twirled a knife in her hand—the knife she'd taken from Ethan's cottage before we stepped through the time portal. As Chronos had explained to us, nothing could exist in two places at once. Anything taken through time would replace the version of it that existed in the past—which was why Ethan's knife had vanished from his hand after we'd stepped through the portal with the same knife from the future.

"Looking for this?" Danielle asked, giving the knife a dramatic swish.

"My knife." Ethan ran for her, but then he stopped. Apparently he realized that despite his strength, he would be at a huge disadvantage in a fight against the three of us without a weapon.

Blake took the opportunity to jump on him from behind, landing a few more punches and capturing Ethan in a hold. But Ethan—a demigod son of Zeus—was stronger than Blake, and it didn't take him long to fight his way free. He ran out of the hold, turning around and breathing heavily to get his bearings. He looked at Blake, and then Danielle, and then at me, defeat crossing his eyes.

"You beat me." He held his hands up, glancing at the top of the mountain. "Put your weapons down, and we'll talk this out. There has to be a compromise we can agree on." He wiped sweat off his forehead and glanced at the cloudy, amber sky again, squinting his eyes as if he were searching for something.

"Looking for Helios's solar dragons?" Danielle asked him.

Ethan whipped his head back to look at her, his

eyebrows scrunched in confusion. "How do you know that…?" he asked, taking a step toward her and looking around. "Where exactly did you come from?"

"*How* I know that doesn't matter," she answered. "What matters is that we have it on good authority that those dragons won't be coming."

"You're wrong," Ethan said, although his voice wavered, his confidence waning.

Blake joined Danielle and me and removed his knife from his boot. "We should bring Ethan back to Kinsley and lock him in the holding room where we kept the siren," he said. "Then we can get to the bottom of all of this and figure out what he knows."

"No." I shook my head, not looking away from Ethan. An image passed through my mind—Blake, in a puddle of his own blood, dead at Ethan's hands. "He's too much of a risk to have around. There's only one way to make sure he doesn't interfere in our mission or hurt any of us ever again."

I pulled back on the string of my bow and shot the arrow straight through Ethan's heart.

CHAPTER TWO

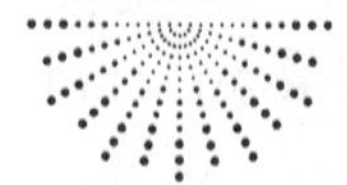

Ethan's eyes glazed over, and he fell to the ground, dead.

I slung my bow around my back and turned to Blake, wrapping him in a hug and crushing my lips against his.

"Blake," I said his name, so happy that he was here, alive. I kissed him again, needing to remind myself that this was real. He kissed me back, but more hesitant, as if he were confused about my sudden enthusiasm.

I supposed I couldn't blame him. It had been only minutes since he'd seen me last. It had been *days* since I'd seen him. And only recently, I didn't think I would ever be able to see him again. The image of him dead would never stop haunting my mind, but he was here. He was alive.

Everything that had happened the first time we were in Kerberos was one long nightmare. And with Ethan dead, it would never become our reality.

After knowing what he did to Blake—or what he *would* do to Blake—I didn't even feel bad about killing Ethan.

I was just happy that Blake was here and Ethan was gone.

I pulled back to look into Blake's eyes, needing to reassure myself that this was actually happening. "I love you, Blake," I said, unable to stop the words from pouring out of my mouth. "I love you so much."

I'd waited too long to say it because I was afraid he might not say it back. If my original timeline had stayed the way it was, I *never* would have gotten the chance to tell him how I felt. Which was why I'd done it now.

I didn't know what would happen in the future. But I knew one thing—I didn't want to have any regrets.

He smiled at me, his familiar brown eyes looking down at me as he traced his finger across my cheek. "I love you, too," he said, and I pulled him closer, relief rushing through my veins at the confirmation that he returned my feelings. "I was waiting for the right time to tell you, but you beat me to it."

"I couldn't wait any longer," I told him. "What if that moment in the cave was the last time we ever saw each other? I couldn't live with that. And now that we're finally with each other again… I didn't want to waste any time. We never know what moment might be our last."

"What's gotten into you?" he asked, smiling. "You're acting like you haven't seen me in a month."

"Not quite a month," I said. "More like a week. But it was the most awful week you could ever imagine…" Memories of my time in Kerberos passed through my mind so quickly that I didn't know where to begin. How could anyone understand what a nightmare it had been without experiencing it for themselves?

"Now's not the time to get into that," Danielle broke into our conversation. "We need to get out of Kerberos. Plus, Chris and Apollo are back on Earth right now with our past selves. Wait until we're there to explain what happened, so you don't have to tell the story more times than necessary."

"Okay," I said, since as always, Danielle had a solid point.

"Your 'past selves?'" Blake repeated, his eyes wide as he looked back and forth between Danielle and me. "And you've met Apollo?"

"It's a long story." I reached for his hand and squeezed it. He squeezed back, although he still looked confused. "But yes, Apollo's on the other side of the portal right now, gifting us with items that will help us on our journey through Kerberos. I'll explain everything soon. For now, let's get back to Earth, okay?"

"I'm getting the feeling that whatever happened to the two of you is crazier than anything I could imagine," he said.

"Your feeling's right." Danielle marched to the portal, but she turned around, looking wistfully up at the mountain.

I knew she wasn't going to miss it here in Kerberos, so there was only one person she could be thinking about—Erebus.

"He'll be fine," I told her. "Remember how easily he pulverized that dragon?"

"I wasn't worried about him," Danielle said. "Of course he'll be fine. He's a primordial deity. I just…" She took a deep breath and tossed her hair over her shoulder, refocusing on me. "It doesn't matter. Are we going back through that portal or what?"

"This story is sounding crazier by the second," Blake muttered.

"You have no idea," I agreed.

We walked to Danielle's side, Blake's hand not leaving mine. I reached for Danielle's hand with my free one, and together, the three of us stepped through the portal.

CHAPTER THREE

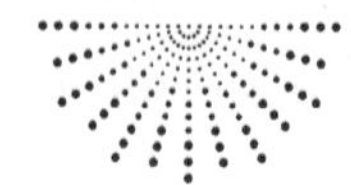

Unlike the first time I'd stepped through the portal to Kerberos, this time I was prepared for the loss of my senses—for the feeling of floating through nothingness. The first time I'd traveled through this portal, I'd panicked. But compared to the portal that had taken me back in time, it was an absolute breeze.

I landed on the ground of the cave, Blake and Danielle's hands still in mine. Apollo stood ahead of us, his back toward us as he presented the Golden Sword to Danielle. The past versions of Chris and myself stood next to her.

But then the past versions of Danielle and me were gone. Vanished into thin air, as if they'd never existed at all. The only thing that remained was the Golden Sword of Athena, which clattered to the ground.

"Whoa." Chris stared at the three of us, then at the empty spots next to him, and then back at us. "How…? When…?" He continued to stare at us, his eyes wide, clearly at a loss for words. "Does anyone want to tell me what's going on here?"

Apollo turned around, his lips curving into a small smile. "Welcome back, Blake," he said. "And Nicole and Danielle… I see you've received help from Chronos."

"Yes." I nodded and glanced at the bag by Apollo's feet. Since I held the Golden Bow in my hand, the version that he'd brought to give to me would be gone. But I hadn't brought the crystal arrows back with me. Were they still in that bag?

"Chronos rarely changes the past himself, let alone allows others to travel through a time portal on their own." Apollo pressed his lips together, studying us. "I can only imagine that whatever happened to you in Kerberos was very grave."

"You have no idea." Danielle walked to the Golden Sword and picked it up, holding it in the air and smiling. "I'm glad to have this back, though." She sheathed the sword, and then she held her palms up to the ceiling, rain showering all around her. She lifted her face to the rain, her expression one of pure bliss. "I'm glad to be able to do that again too," she said once the rain shower stopped.

I gathered white energy, healing all the bug bites, stings, scratches, and every other injury that I'd gotten during my time in Kerberos. "I can use my power again, too." I reached for Blake to heal him—he'd gotten pretty banged up in his fight with Ethan—and walked over to do the same for Danielle. It felt amazing to access the white energy again—as if a part of myself had been restored.

"What's going on here?" Chris asked. "You were both standing next to me, and then suddenly you were gone and coming through the portal with Blake. You're all dirty and look like you've been through hell. Where did you go? And why am I the only one left here?"

"They received help from Chronos—the primordial deity of time itself," Apollo explained. "How far in the future are you from?"

"Not long," I told him. "We were only in Kerberos for a week."

"Except for me," Blake added. "I was there for minutes, at the most."

"True," I said. "It was Danielle and I who were there for a few days. Then we came back, saved Blake and Medusa's head, and came back through the portal."

"What happened during the week you were in Kerberos?" Apollo asked.

"A *lot*." I shuddered at the memories, not wanting to think about them any more than necessary. "Maybe we should explain starting from this moment, when you gave us the gifts the first time around?"

"Yes." Apollo nodded. "Please do."

"I'll summarize as fast as I can, since we only have a week before Typhon rises, and we need to figure out how to stop him," I said. "After you gave us our gifts, we —me, Danielle, and Chris—entered the portal to Kerberos. When we got there, Blake and Ethan were being flown up the mountain by Helios's solar dragons. We tried to climb directly up the mountain to get to them, but it was too dangerous, so we had to find another way."

"There were tons of wildlife on the mountain trying to kill us," Danielle added. "Including the Nemean lion. Even with our weapons, we wouldn't have made it up the mountain alive."

"Did we even *try* to fight them?" Chris asked. "I can't imagine that we would give up without trying."

"Yes," I told him. "We killed a bunch of huge foxes. But you got bit on the shoulder in the process. We didn't know it at the time, but the venom was poisonous. And since we didn't have access to our elemental powers while we were in Kerberos, I couldn't heal you."

"So... I died?" His eyes widened, his expression serious. "That's why I didn't come back through the time portal with you?"

"Not exactly," I said. "The venom would have taken weeks to make its way through your system. It *is* why you're not here, but I want to tell this story in order, so I'll get back to that part later."

"Okay." Chris nodded. "Go ahead."

"After seeing the lions, we turned back to find another way up the mountain," I said. "That was when Erebus found us."

"Of course Erebus gets his kicks out of wandering the hell dimension." Apollo rolled his eyes. "Hopefully he didn't give you much trouble. Since you're still alive, I'm guessing he didn't."

"He was there to help us." Danielle raised her chin, matching Apollo's gaze. "We wouldn't have made it out of Kerberos alive without Erebus there as our guide. We owe him our lives."

"Sorry." Apollo held his hands out in apology, although his voice dripped with sarcasm. "I didn't realize the two of you were so close."

Danielle glared at him and said nothing.

"Anyway," I said, wanting to break the tension between them. "Erebus led us along another, more meandering path that led us to a safer way up the mountain. We faced a lot of trials along the journey—every realm in Kerberos was designed to torture us or kill us—but eventually we made it to the Lair of the Dragons. Since the mountain becomes too steep to climb past that point, we made a deal with the dragons to fly us up the mountain."

"Dragons are notoriously difficult to bargain with," Apollo said. "What did you offer them to get them to agree?"

"The Golden Sword of Athena." Danielle ran her fingers along the handle of the sword, and I knew she was glad to have it back.

"Ah." Apollo nodded. "An offer they couldn't refuse."

"By that point, the Golden Lyre was out of tune, and I only had one crystal arrow left," I explained. "The Golden Sword was all we had that they wanted. So they took it, and they flew us up the mountain. There was a frozen lake at the peak, with the Titans trapped inside. They couldn't do anything to harm us—I don't think they were even aware that we were there—but the ice was starting to crack. Once it cracks, they'll be able to break free."

"You need to close the portal before that happens," Apollo said, his eyes more intense than I'd seen them yet.

"Yes," I agreed. "We know."

"Where was I through all of this?" Blake asked. "You said that those dragons had flown Ethan and me up that same mountain, right? Were we still there when you got there?"

I met his eyes and opened my mouth to tell him, but I couldn't. How did you tell someone that they'd been murdered? Even though it had happened in another timeline, I didn't think I could speak the words without breaking down from the memory of finding his bloodied corpse in the center of that cottage. Just remembering it now was enough to make me re-live the grief all over again.

He watched me closely, resolve crossing over his features. "I didn't make it," he said, his voice strangely calm for such a strong revelation. "Did I?"

"You couldn't access your powers in Kerberos, and it was you against Ethan and the two dragons," I told him. "Ethan didn't even *need* to bring you with him—all he wanted was Medusa's head. He only took you so he could kill you and cause me the same grief that he'd had to go through when Rachael died."

"That twisted monster," Blake growled, his fists clenched to his sides. "Now I understand why you didn't let him live back in Kerberos. If you hadn't killed him already, I would do it myself."

"I had no choice," I agreed. "I had to kill him."

But even though I said it, there was still a part of me that questioned what I'd done. Because I *did* have a choice.

And I'd chosen to kill him.

The scary thing was—I didn't regret it.

"So Blake was dead and Chris was poisoned," Apollo said, bringing us back to the story. "It still doesn't seem like enough incentive to get Chronos to send you through a time portal."

Even though he was my father, I wanted to tell him that he was a jerk for saying that so insensitively. Sure, Blake and Chris were fine now, but he had no idea how torn apart we'd been when we thought otherwise.

But I held my tongue, because he was right. Both of those things *weren't* what convinced Chronos to send us through the portal.

"Ethan also destroyed Medusa's head," I explained. "He gouged out her eyes, making them useless."

"And without Medusa's head, the group of you had no chance against Typhon," Apollo concluded.

"Exactly," Danielle said. "So even though I figured it was a long shot, I asked Erebus if he could contact Chronos for us. He did, and after realizing that the world would end if the timeline remained as it was, Chronos came to us and created a time portal so we could go back and change the past."

"Why did you go back to a point where you could save Blake, but not Kate?" Chris clenched his fists, looking at Danielle and me like we were monsters. "Did you forget about her completely?"

"Of course not!" I said, hating that he thought that for even a second. "The first thing I asked was if we could go back to before the fight with Medusa so we could save Kate. But Chronos wouldn't allow it. He refused to send us back that far because he wouldn't risk the outcome of the fight changing, and us not getting Medusa's head. *He* decided on the point when we returned. We didn't have a say."

"Okay," Chris said, although he still looked uneasy. "So why didn't I come back with you? Was that bite I'd gotten from the fox so bad that I would have been a detriment when you returned to fight Ethan?"

"Mortals aren't meant to travel through time," Danielle explained. "Doing so causes a huge stress to our bodies—it takes away one year of our natural lives. Nicole couldn't heal you since she couldn't access her powers, and because of the bite, you only had weeks left to live. If you'd gone through the time portal, you wouldn't have survived."

"It's probably good that you don't have to remember anything," I added. "What we went through in Kerberos... the things we saw while there... I wish I could go back to before it all and never have to experience it, too."

"I don't," Danielle said. "Everything we go through in our lives—even the hard parts—helps make us who we are. I wouldn't forget anything, even if I could."

I suspected that she just didn't want to forget *Erebus*, but the situation was too intense to joke about, so I said nothing.

"I guess I understand why I couldn't come back with you," Chris said. "But what happened to the version of me that traveled with you through Kerberos? He was just... left behind?"

"As Chronos explained it, the version of you from that timeline ceased to exist the moment we traveled back here and changed the past," I said. "That timeline is gone. You—*this* version of you—is the only one that's real."

"This is heavy." Chris sighed and ran his hand through his hair.

"It is," Apollo agreed. "It's best not to overthink time travel too much, or it will make your head spin. What matters is that your mission to Kerberos was successful and that you're home safely. I was just preparing to give you your gifts, but since you don't need them anymore, they won't be necessary."

"But you're not taking back the sword." Danielle's hand flew protectively to its handle. "Right?"

"No." Apollo chuckled. "The Golden Sword was yours to begin with, so I wouldn't dream of taking it back. And Nicole, you can keep the Golden Bow that you brought back with you, too."

"And the crystal arrows?" I asked, motioning toward the bag. "They're in there, right?"

"They are." He nodded. "And I'm glad to know that they were helpful to you while you were in Kerberos. But crystal arrows aren't exactly easy to come by. And now that you're back, you don't need them anymore. So I'll be holding onto them until they're needed in the future."

"It's too bad we won't be getting our gifts." Chris pouted. "I love getting presents. I was looking forward to seeing what mine would be."

"Nicole or Danielle can tell you later," Apollo said. "For now, there are more important issues to discuss."

"Like what?" I asked.

"I have information that's supposed to be secret to you," he said. "You're supposed to figure it out on your own. But I believe that you deserve a reward for succeeding in your mission through Kerberos, and this information will help you defeat Typhon… so now, I will tell you what you need to know."

ABOUT THE AUTHOR

Michelle Madow is a *USA Today* bestselling author of fantasy romance novels filled with forbidden love, elemental magic, and epic twists that readers never see coming. With over three million books sold and translations in multiple languages, her addictive stories have captured hearts around the world.

She wrote her first novel in college and never looked

back. Now, with 50 books published (and counting), she spends her time dreaming up magical realms and devastating romances that keep readers hooked from page one.

Originally from Maryland, she spent nearly two decades in Florida before a brief chapter in NYC—and now she's back in the Sunshine State, where golden days fuel her creativity and moonlight sparks her imagination.

When she's not writing, she's likely getting lost in the magical world of reading, plotting her next big twist, or reminiscing about her travels to all seven continents.

Never miss a new release by signing up to get emails or texts when Michelle's books come out:

Sign up for emails: michellemadow.com/subscribe
Sign up for texts: michellemadow.com/texts

Connect with Michelle:

Instagram: @michellemadow
TikTok: @michellemadow
Facebook: facebook.com/MichLMadow
Email: michelle@michellemadow.com

www.ingramcontent.com/pod-product-compliance
Lightning Source LLC
Chambersburg PA
CBHW020912310726
48980CB00011B/848/J

* 9 7 8 0 5 7 8 9 8 8 5 9 7 *